Number one Albert Square was a sturdy-looking end-of-terrace house, tall and narrow, with steps leading up to the main entrance and down to the basement door. It faced one end of the square's central garden, and it was close to the Victorian pub on the corner of Bridge Street.

'What do you think?' Harold asked Judith.

'It looks fine, from the outside. But so did the last one.' They walked around the side and looked over the wall surrounding the garden. 'There's a window open,' Judith observed.

'Oh, yes, so there is. I think we'll stick to the conventional method of entry, though.' He checked the list. 'Keys with landlord, Queen Victoria public house.'

By the same author

The Outsider
The Dark Side of the Sun

EastEnders Novels

Swings and Roundabouts

HUGH MILLER

Home Fires Burning

EastEnders – Book 1

By arrangement with the British Broadcasting Corporation

GRAFTON BOOKS
A Division of the Collins Publishing Group

LONDON GLASGOW
TORONTO SYDNEY AUCKLAND

Grafton Books
A Division of the Collins Publishing Group
8 Grafton Street, London W1X 3LA

Published by Grafton Books 1985

EastEnders copyright © BBC 1985
This novel copyright © Hugh Miller, Julia Smith
and Tony Holland 1985

ISBN 0-586-06809-0

Printed and bound in Great Britain by
Collins, Glasgow

Set in Times

All rights reserved. No part of this publication may
be reproduced, stored in a retrieval system, or
transmitted, in any form, or by any means, electronic,
mechanical, photocopying, recording or otherwise,
without the prior permission of the publishers.

This book is sold subject to the conditions that it
shall not, by way of trade or otherwise, be lent,
re-sold, hired out or otherwise circulated
without the publisher's prior consent in any
form of binding or cover other than that in
which it is published and without a similar
condition including this condition being imposed
on the subsequent purchaser.

ACKNOWLEDGEMENT

I am indebted to Joe and Una Caulfield
who provided valuable research
material

1

'Last night,' Alvar Liddell said, 'the Admiralty and the Air Ministry issued the first full account of the Atlantic battle and pursuit which ended, at one minute past eleven yesterday morning, in the sinking of the *Bismarck*, the finest fighting ship in Hitler's fleet.'

Albert Beale turned from the window and switched off the wireless. 'Third time I've heard that today,' he grunted. He glanced at Louise. 'What's up, love?' She had stopped in the middle of what she was doing, her hands resting on a pile of old woollens in a box on the table. She was staring at her mother's picture, the only thing left on the sideboard. 'Lou?'

'Nothing.' She shook back a strand of hair and threw a couple of folded jumpers into the box. 'Just thinking, that's all.'

'And bottling it all up.' Albert came across and put a hand on her shoulder. 'You'll feel different soon.'

'Worse, I shouldn't doubt.'

Louise pushed the box away from her and gazed round the living room. With the beds and rugs gone and the other furniture stacked against one wall, it looked a lot bigger than she'd believed it could. Bigger and sadder.

'Never thought I'd be sorry to leave this place,' she murmured. 'Now it's come to it, I don't want to go.' She gulped and a tear shone.

'Now then, now then,' Albert breathed soothingly. 'Don't go getting yourself in a state.'

She stared at him the way she often did lately. It was as if she was engraving his face on her memory, dwelling on the big serious grey eyes, the quiff of sandy hair that always lay on his forehead, his mouth that never quite seemed to lose its smile.

'There's lots to be thankful for,' he said.

Louise shook her head. 'It just don't seem fair. None of it.'

Albert drew her close, comforting her, sparing her the sight of his own small, anxious frown. He knew well enough why Lou didn't want to quit these bleak old rooms; leaving would be the first acknowledgement of change – change brought on by loss and the spectre of separation. Their lives were taking a new direction, a road full of shadowy uncertainties.

'Dwelling on things doesn't help, my love.' He squeezed her shoulders. 'If you've got to have something to think about, just keep reminding yourself you're going to have your very own house. No more sharing.'

Louise nodded with her face pressed to his chest.

'Tell you what.' Albert eased back gently and smiled at her. 'I'll make us a brew while you finish in here. We can drink it to cheer us up while we're waiting for the rent man.'

Louise made her own effort at a smile. 'Just the ticket,' she said, turning away quickly and attacking the box again.

On his way along the hall Albert peeped into the big black pram by the stairs. Young Ronnie was sound asleep with his thumb jammed in his mouth. Albert nudged his foreboding aside and conferred a swift silent blessing on his son. As he moved on to the tiny kitchen he heard his eldest, Harry, outside in the yard yelling at one of his little mates.

'It's your turn to be the Jerry! I was him last time – an' I got flamin' killed, an' all!'

The war had been official for less than two years, but

its influence on all their lives was so total, so enveloping, that it seemed to have been with them for an age. Ten months before, when the Germans had moved their pressure from the military targets and began bombing Poplar, Stepney, Walford and West Ham, the ferocity of Blitzkrieg became a shattering reality for the Beales and everyone else in the East End. Adults lived with daily anxiety, fright and recurrent tragedy. The children no longer played at cowboys and Indians.

'Shitty war,' Albert muttered as he fished the battered caddy from the box of packets and tins behind the door. He prised open the lid and then paused with the spoon in his hand, thinking again about his call-up papers – their formal brevity, their finality. Even though he had been expecting them, he'd been scared when he saw the words WAR DEPARTMENT and realized what had dropped on the doormat. He was glad no one had been there to see his face.

Three days had given him time to regard his conscription with less raw-nerved distress. He had managed, in fact, to muster a fair measure of acceptance. It was easy to compare that moment with the envelope trembling in his hand to the way he felt now, standing in the cubbyhole kitchen spooning tea-leaves into the pot. He was achingly conscious of his wife and children, of how precious they were to him, how vulnerable. They were targets in this filthy war, so he could take old Hitler's aggression very personally; anger would come to his rescue whenever he got scared again. He could even imagine himself squaring-up to a storm-trooper or two, bare-handed.

There was a tap on the door. 'Spare a cup for a parched soul down on his luck, mate?' Albert turned and saw Terence, Louise's second-oldest brother, a short, glossy-haired young man with constantly mobile eyes and a pencil moustache which he refused to shave off, even though it was the focus of steady derision from his family. 'I let meself in the back way, Albert.' He patted a bulging paper bag tucked under his arm. 'Brought you a handful of this and that, if you're interested.' He winked, instantly explaining how he had come by the goods.

Albert shook his head. 'Beats me how you sleep at night.'

'No problem,' Terence assured him. He edged in and put the bag on the ledge by the sink. 'Way I look at it, I'm a Samaritan. Helpin' others in need.'

'More of a bloody Robin Hood,' Albert observed. 'Except you *sell* to the poor.'

Terence affected hurt. 'Where else would you get the little luxuries in life if it wasn't for the likes of me?' he demanded. 'And I mean, I do shell-out for the stuff, don't I? It's not as if I nicked it or nothing. A little commission's all I ask, in view of the effort an' risk.'

'Yeah, well . . .' Albert was in no mood to discuss the ethics of his brother-in-law's enterprise. 'Let's have a look at what you've got.'

Terence made some show of unrolling the top of the bag, as if a sudden outrush of splendour might blind the pair of them. His traffic with the Black Market had been casual and tentative in the early days, but by now he had the mark of the professional. He could be found regularly in pubs and at the back doors of relatives and acquaintances, hunched over his wares and delivering a sales chat that involved scarcely any movement of his lips.

'How about that, then?' He pulled out a tin with *Gold Flake* printed on the side and held it under Albert's nose. 'The ideal smoke for all kinds of folk. There's a hundred and twenty vacuum-packed fags in there.'

'How much?'

'Four and a tanner.'

'They'd be nearer three and a tanner in the shops.'

'When did the shops last have them?'

Albert sighed and nodded. Terence put down the cigarettes and produced a tube of toothpaste. 'Gibbs SR. Saves your teeth because it's good for your gums.'

'I can do without the adverts, Terry. How much?'

'It's the sixpenny size – you can have it for sevenpence ha'penny. If you take three, that is.'

The pile by the sink grew swiftly. There were two tins of oranges, three bars of Lifebuoy toilet soap, a pair of Bondor fully-fashioned silk stockings – 'Eight and eleven, Albert, but it's a rarity I'm offering you here, right?' – a bottle of sweet white wine, four tins of Ovaltine and a big box of Pond's non-detectable face powder.

'And now, because you're family and because I'm a mug for not hangin' on to them meself . . .' Slowly, Terence pulled a one-pound box of Cadbury's Milk Tray from the bottom of the bag and held it before Albert like a trophy. 'When did you last see these, eh?' He stroked the box reverently. 'Year ago? Two years? And these ain't old stock, Albert, they're fresh, straight out of the wholesalers this very week.'

Albert was suspicious. 'I thought they'd stopped making them.'

'No, no.' Terence narrowed one eye. 'For the likes of us, there's them titchy little bars with the extra iron in. But the nobs can still lay their hands on these. All I've done is laid my hands on some of theirs – just so's you and our Lou can sit by the fire an' munch up a few memories.' He slapped the box and held it tantalizingly nearer. 'Half a dollar and I'm robbing meself.'

Albert nodded. As he recollected, the chocolates had been a shilling a pound the last time he'd bought any – but Lou enjoyed nothing better than getting tucked into some soft centres. 'Add it all up and I'll settle with you before you go.'

'Right. This is the way to do business, eh?'

The kettle was boiling. Albert filled the teapot and put on the lid. 'Tuppence a cup be all right?' he enquired softly.

Terence slapped his arm and offered him a cigarette from a silver-plated case. 'Heard about your call-up,' he said, watching Albert's glum reaction as he gave him a light. 'I thought you'd be safe. Like me.'

'Well . . .' Albert drew heavily on the cigarette and exhaled the smoke with a sigh. 'They keep changing the rules, don't they? They'll maybe even catch you, some day.'

Terence had a defective heart valve that had earned him a disabled classification. In Albert's case, the disability was a scarred eardrum – the result of a childhood infection – which, until a recent revision of the conscription standards, had meant he wasn't eligible for war service.

'I'd shoot me soddin' knees off sooner than go,' Terence said with some feeling.

'You might have to. From what I've heard, you only need to be warm to wind up in uniform these days.' Albert sighed again, swirling the teapot. 'Less than two weeks and I'll be off.'

'How's Lou takin' it?'

'She's bitter. Who wouldn't be? Barely a month since the old lady passed on, and now this.'

Terence shrugged. 'We'll just have to rally round a bit and get her to count her blessings.'

'I've been making an effort in that direction.'

Albert lined up the cups and began pouring. He had put the arguments plainly to Lou, trying to give her a blueprint for optimism. Six years of marriage, he had reminded her, and four sturdy kids had given them a warmth and solidarity that was twenty-two carat. They would have a home of their own, now Gran was gone and they were inheriting her council house; it was a place where roots could be set deep and the kids would grow up happy and unhindered. *And* they were still a young couple, weren't they? Lou was only 26, Albert barely four years older. It all added up to hope and reassurance, he had insisted.

But the credit side of their circumstances did nothing to cheer Lou. Where was the closeness and warmth in being separated for God-knows how long, with no guarantee you would ever see each other again? As for having a home of their own, she would have been happy to do without it, just to have her mum around a few more years – especially years when there would be no husband to give her love or comfort or damn-all else. To put the gloss on her misery, she would be left to look after the children and run the fruit and vegetable stall on her own.

'She's not a happy girl, Terence,' Albert murmured as they went through to the living room. He elbowed the door open and smiled broadly at Louise, who was tying string round two carrier bags crammed with clothes. 'Here's your cuppa, sweetheart.'

'Ta.' Louise took the cup and glanced at Terence. 'What're you doing here?'

'Brought round a few things,' he said. 'Some nice little specials. You'll be pleased I did – right, Albert?'

'Got you some chocolates,' Albert said. 'The real McCoy.'

Lou sipped her tea. 'We better eat the evidence quick as we can, then, before the law gets here.'

Terence accepted Albert's eye-warning and said nothing. He gulped his tea instead, surveying the stacked furniture, the rows of paper bags and boxes.

'About ready for the off then, aren't we,' Albert

observed, just to fill the silence. Lou's mood was fragile, and the presence of her least favourite brother didn't help. She was setting up one of her atmospheres.

'Movin' today, then?' Terence asked.

'You're the only one of the family that isn't lendin' a hand, far as I know,' Louise muttered. She put her cup on the window ledge and hoisted the carrier bags on to a stack of boxes.

'We're just waiting for the rent man,' Albert explained. 'Got to get it all sorted out legal an' that before we move in.'

As Louise picked up her cup again they heard familiar shuffling footsteps on the hall linoleum. 'Talk of the devil,' she murmured, staring accusingly at the door. From her expression she might have been expecting the bailiffs.

'In here, Mr Emmett,' Albert called. He flashed a little frown at Louise, warning her not to be short with the old man. It wasn't the rent collector's fault that he was about to start the ball rolling on a future she'd have done anything to defer.

The door swung inwards and a stooped, balding man in a shiny serge suit came into the room. He acknowledged the others with a nod for each and then added another nod at the furniture. 'All set, eh?'

'That's right,' Albert said, rubbing his hands nervously. 'How are you keeping, Mr Emmett? I heard you'd had 'flu.'

Emmett shrugged, fishing in his inside pocket. 'Might 'ave been that. Just felt rotten for a week or two.' He gave a rattling sigh. 'Tubes, joints, giblets – all a bit ropey these days. Old age don't arrive on its todd, I can tell you.'

'True enough,' Terence chirped.

The rent man shot him a kind of look he saved for

cheeky kids, then he produced a small green book and held it out to Louise. 'There it is, then,' he said. 'You're all properly registered and the first week's rent's been entered – it's in your name, love.'

Louise took the rent book and stared at it. Under the crest of the London Borough of Walford was written the address that had been her mother's for so many years – 45, Albert Square. Under that was written the name of the new tenant, oldest of her family and therefore natural successor, Louise Ada Beale.

'I hope you'll have a lot of happy years there,' Emmett said. 'All of you.'

Louise looked up at him, her small round face suddenly blank and childlike. She glanced at Albert.

'I'm sure we will,' he said, tightening an arm round Lou's shoulder, feeling the tremor as she clutched Emmett's gift and fought back her tears.

2

'1941 could be the most significant year of the war,' Mike Phillips said as they strode along the echoing corridor towards the Emergency Room. 'And almost certainly the last.'

Beside him Harold Legg shrugged. 'Could be,' he murmured.

'Now the *Bismarck*'s been scuppered, it's only a matter of time before the whole dashed German navy goes under.'

'Scuppered's when you do it intentionally to your own ship,' Harold pointed out.

'I don't want to split hairs,' Phillips snapped. 'The plain fact is, the whole Nazi war plan is falling apart. They're just not up to their own ambitions.'

Phillips was a gangly, short-sighted youth with widely spaced teeth, thin oily hair and sallow skin; at nineteen, he gave the impression of having been born middle-aged. He read the *Daily Telegraph* six days a week and quoted from it at every opportunity – although he preferred people to believe that the opinions, forecasts and verdicts he spouted were all his own.

'I think the Nazis are more than up to their ambitions,' Harold Legg said. He pushed his way through a crowd of students by the door to a lecture theatre, deliberately leaving Phillips struggling behind him. He sprinted along the passage and into Emergency, grabbing a white coat and mask as he went. The mask wasn't strictly necessary, but it might make him anonymous enough to escape Phillips' attention for a while.

'Ah. Legg. Follow me.' The plump figure of Dr Lumley paused just long enough to beckon Harold then he waddled on, leading the way among the stretchers and trolleys crowding the high, wide room that had been set aside for serious bombing casualties. Harold followed, giving up the attempt to hook the mask over his ears.

'Another seventeen admitted in the last hour,' Lumley called over his shoulder. 'An unexploded bomb buried in rubble, apparently. Went off just after seven and flattened a row of houses. Blew the side out of a warehouse, too. The night shift were still inside.'

The mingling cries of the injured and the odours of burnt clothing, hair and flesh assailed Harold as he hurried along behind the old Consultant. At trolleys and wheeled beds doctors and nurses worked in teams of two and three, stitching wounds, bracing fractures, administering blood and drugs. At one trolley a nurse held down a screaming baby while another removed splinters of glass from its face and head. Alongside, two doctors attended an old woman who had lost an eye. A man lay on a table beyond her, wide-eyed with pain, groaning through clenched teeth as a doctor prepared to work on his mangled leg. The foot had been almost severed at the ankle, and along the calf white shards of bone jutted through torn skin and muscle.

Dr Lumley stopped and knelt by a stretcher on the floor. 'Come and look at this, Legg.'

Harold approached and leaned close, smelling something like paint. The patient was a young man with deep cuts on his face and scalp. He was unconscious. Dr Lumley drew back the sheet from his body. There were perhaps fifty wounds on his chest and upper arms; on at least half of them the skin hung in flaps.

'A canister of white spirit exploded all over him. The

wounds are full of debris – brick dust, fragments of metal, wood splinters, glass.'

'You want me to clean them,' Harold said, already looking around for an instrument tray he could use.

'Menial work, I know,' Dr Lumley grunted as he stood up. 'But always remember, Legg, it's vital. You're saving people from disfigurement and long-term infection.'

'I don't mind doing it, Doctor.' That week Harold had already picked, swabbed and washed the fragments from hundreds of wounds on dozens of patients. First-year medical students were seldom given anything else to do in Emergency. Before the war, he wouldn't have been allowed to touch a patient at all until late in his second year, so he counted the experience a bonus.

'Do a thorough job, lad, and as quickly as you can – there's a lot of suturing to be done and the blood supply's poor in some of those flaps.'

'Very well, sir.'

'I've given him a morphine injection, so he won't be any trouble. I'll send a nurse to help you, if I can find a spare one.' Dr Lumley turned and waddled away to the rear doors, where more casualties were being brought in.

Harold dug around on a supplies table and found a sterile pack with kidney basin, forceps, swabs, distilled water and antiseptic. He knelt with it beside the patient and began to work.

Only one cut had been cleared before he was interrupted by Mike Phillips, who stopped at the opposite side of the stretcher and frowned at him.

'What's up?' Harold asked.

'I'm puzzled, frankly.'

Harold nodded slowly. 'It can be a puzzling game, medicine.'

'It's you I'm puzzled by.'

Harold sighed. 'Spit it out, Mike, I'm busy here.'

'What did you mean when you said you think the Nazis are more than up to their ambitions?'

'I meant just what I said.' Harold stared at him, taking in the spread feet, the folded arms and the scowl of offended nationalism. When he was younger he had seen the identical stance and expression on black-shirted men in the East End. 'The Nazis' ambitions aren't primarily about waging wars,' he said. 'They've gone a long way already towards achieving what they really want. They're *very* capable in that direction.'

Phillips' eyes wavered. War tactics and simple, uncomplicated patriotism were his territory. On political and moral issues he was as much a virgin as he was sexually. 'I'd hate to think you found something to admire about them,' he said lamely, shifting his feet.

'I admire nothing about them, Mike. Now do you mind? This fellow needs my attention a lot more than you do.'

For another ten minutes Harold worked on the patient, assiduously removing dirt and irrigating the tissue until the strain of his kneeling position forced him to stop. As he stood up, rubbing his back, a porter came across and told him there was a free trolley. They hoisted the stretcher on to it and Harold began to work again. As he did a nurse approached.

'Mr Legg?'

Harold paused and looked at her. He was over six feet tall, so most people looked small to him. But this girl was truly small, a compact little figure with dark brown hair and eyes like burnt amber. She looked almost too young and fragile, too *innocent*, to be standing in the midst of such hideous sights and terrible odours. Yet she looked perfectly calm and confident. Noticing a twinkle of amusement, Harold suddenly realized he was staring. 'Ah – yes, Mr Legg, that's me.'

'Dr Lumley sent me to give you a hand.'

'Oh. Right. Marvellous.' He dithered for a moment then went to the supplies table and brought back another pack. 'Don't suppose you need me to tell you what to do,' he mumbled, handing it over. He stood and watched as she tore off the wrapper and organized the contents by the side of the patient. Her hands were very dainty, he noticed, and she moved them so elegantly. The nails were superbly shaped, like flawless, miniature almonds . . .

God! he thought; *I'm staring again!*

As they worked, Harold on one side of the patient, the nurse on the other, he tried to think of something to say. Oddly, nothing casual enough would come to mind. He was still trying when the girl spoke up.

'How long have you been at Bart's, Mr Legg?'

'A year,' he said, clearing his throat. 'Have you been here long?'

'Eleven months.'

Fearing they had hit a dead end already, Harold voiced the first thing that flew to mind. 'We must be about the same age.' He took a glance at her. 'I'm nineteen,' he volunteered.

'So am I.'

In the further few minutes it took to finish cleaning the patient's wounds, they managed to exchange a good deal of information. Harold learned that the nurse was from Fulham and that her father was an assistant manager at a bank in Chelsea. She liked nursing and wanted to do midwifery and orthopaedics after she'd completed her general training. In her spare time she played tennis, read books and helped her mother on a committee for rehabilitating the war-homeless.

Harold revealed that he was originally from the East End, though the family had moved to Finchley some years ago. His father was a specialist in heart diseases, with a private practice and Consultant positions at two hospitals. Harold was passionately keen on medicine; he had volunteered to spend three days a week in Emergency, so he spent most of his so-called free time studying. Eventually, he wanted to have a general practice in the East End. He liked orchestral and chamber music, reading and visiting his uncle Leon, who was a professional musician.

A doctor and a Sister took over as Harold and the nurse finally moved away from the trolley. 'Well, that's that,' he said awkwardly.

'I'll be off, then,' the nurse said. 'I'm overdue at Men's Surgical.' Harold's stomach shifted leadenly as she smiled, nodded farewell and went off smartly towards the ambulance bay.

'Legg!' somebody shouted. He turned and saw Dr Lumley, surrounded by trollies. 'I've got some more for you.'

When he looked back the nurse had gone. He trudged over to Dr Lumley, balefully realizing that for all he'd learned about her, he'd forgotten to ask her name.

Throughout the rest of the morning his mind kept drifting to the girl, picturing her, conjuring her voice and comparing her to the only other person who had moved him so profoundly – Rita Margolis, a neighbour's daughter who had captivated him briefly when he was sixteen.

This was much different, Harold decided. Rita had held him with her pretty pouting, her teasing manner, the occasional coy gesture of affection and, more often, a refusal even to acknowledge his existence whenever there were any other boys around. He blushed for the poor bewitched, tortured clown he had been. That infatuation ended, mercifully if painfully, when he learned that, whenever Rita spoke about him to other girls, she referred to him as 'Big Drippy from next door'.

Thinking of the little nurse, he could never imagine her being anything like Rita. She was open, affable, disarmingly direct. He couldn't believe she would be devious, conniving or anything less than honest in any of her transactions – whether they were social, professional or emotional.

Towards noon, Harold owned up to himself. He was not a young man who hurried to any conclusion, but he was pretty sure that, after three years' of submersion in study, scarcely noticing girls, he was suddenly and profoundly smitten.

He took his lunch break in the hospital canteen. He was surrounded by a democratic mix of other students, fire wardens, porters, nurses, radiographers and doctors. Nowhere among them did he see the little nurse. Distracted, chewing apathetically at his egg-powder omelette and soggy chips, he heard a familiar voice at his ear.

'Your lunch looks like somebody's eaten it once already.'

Harold turned and grinned at Roger Lewis, a bushy-headed second-year student he'd known since their grammar school days at Hackney Downs.

'Squeeze over, will you?' Roger put his bowl of soup and wedge of bread on the table and swung his leg over the bench. As he sat down he groaned melodramatically. 'What a bloody morning.'

'What have you been doing?'

'Finding out how they count the numbers of dead after a bombing. Well, one of the ways.' He shook his head. 'Pre-war medical training could never have been like this.'

Harold had already seen the pulpy chaos of limbs, sundered heads and split torsos littering the site of a direct hit. Even where there were only a few bodies in a particular spot, the devastation was so extreme that it seemed impossible for anyone to determine, even roughly, how many there had been. 'How *do* they count them?'

'They locate all the genitals, remove them and lay them in a line. Pretty reliable method, I'm assured. And it means they can provide separate figures for males and females.'

'Charming.' Harold pushed the stiff segment of omelette around the plate with his fork. 'Care to talk about something else?'

'Horses?'

'Racehorses?'

Roger nodded, slurping his soup.

'I don't know a thing about them.'

'Pity.' Roger tore off a piece of bread and gestured with it. 'Newmarket on Saturday – I've been given three names for the May Two-Year-Old Stakes. I'm assured one of them will win. Wanted a second opinion, so I could maybe narrow it down to two, or even one. I could use a few quid right now.'

'Who gave you the names?'

'A grateful patient over in Medical. I smuggled him in a bag of crushed ice for his piles.' Roger stared thoughtfully at the bread for a moment. 'He's definitely a well-informed old punter, but he played hard to get, you know? Wouldn't narrow it any more for me. For that, I got the impression he'd want a flask of alcohol.'

Harold had never bet on horses, but he was familiar with people who did. Their final selections were invariably made on the basis of superstition or vague associations of names and events. 'What are the horses called?' he asked Roger.

'Cavendish, Cosmo Lass and Gold Nib.'

'Back Gold Nib.'

Roger frowned. 'Why?'

'That fountain pen I lost – it turned up at the bottom of my briefcase this morning.'

'Right,' Roger said assertively. 'That's good enough for me.' He slapped Harold's shoulder and got on with consuming his lunch.

After a minute, when he finally decided to abandon the remains of the omelette and the greasy chips, Harold said, 'Would you like to do me a little favour, in return for guaranteeing your fortune on Saturday?'

Roger munched his bread and swallowed hard. 'Let me guess.' He hammed deep thought for a moment then snapped his fingers. 'Got it. You want me to lay on the alibi when you poison that bastard Phillips.'

Harold smiled. 'Now you mention it, maybe I should settle for that. But no, it's a girl . . .'

'Uh-uh.' Roger shook his head firmly. 'I don't know *anyone* who'll perform special surgery on ladies in pod. And I can't do it myself – I lost my buttonhook.'

'Seriously. There's a nurse, very petite, brown hair and eyes, really delicate looking, like china . . .'

Roger was thinking again, seriously this time. 'Wears a silver fob watch, one of the old-fashioned kind with wispy decorations round the edge?'

As soon as he mentioned it Harold remembered. 'Yes. That's right. Do you know who she is, by any chance? Her name, I mean.'

Roger nodded calmly. 'Yes, I do. Why are you interested in her?'

Harold felt his face grow warm. 'Somebody else is, actually. I said I'd find out, if I could . . .'

'Judith Martin. First-year student, does shuttle auxiliary on Men's Surgical, Women's Medical and Emergency.'

Harold felt very secure, suddenly. With her name he had a line to her, he could make an approach.

'Your friend who's interested,' Roger said, 'I'd tell him not to build up his hopes.'

Harold frowned. 'Why not?'

'She's going out with a houseman from Men's Surgical. Has been for months.' He winked. 'Looks serious.'

'Oh.' Harold stared at the congealed, repugnant tangle of chips on his plate. 'That could be awkward, couldn't it? I'll pass it on. Thanks.'

'Think nothing of it,' Roger said. 'One good turn, and all that.' He waved his hand demonstratively, dripping soup from his bread on to the table. 'What are mates for, anyway?'

3

During the second week of Albert Beale's army service, Louise found that her spirits were steadily brightening. It was hard to say why. She was minding her children, putting the house in shape, doing four mornings a week on the stall and sleeping alone at nights. In prospect it had seemed like a recipe for hardship, unhappiness and exhaustion. In the first week of Albert's absence, she was convinced it would work out just that way, with no hope of improvement.

Albert's going was a wrenching of the spirit that left Louise desolate and tearful. For three days she existed in a state of isolation from her surroundings. She neglected the house and the family and did little more than shuffle around the place clutching a handkerchief or sit by the window, eyes misted, staring. There had been no way to harden herself in advance, no consolation powerful enough to soften her agonizing sense of loss.

Elsie, her twenty-three-year-old sister, was persuaded by the rest of the family to go and stay with Louise for a time. Elsie was reluctant, but she was also single and between jobs, so she didn't have her other sisters' limitations of time and domestic responsibility.

For three days Elsie cleaned the house, cooked and saw to the children's needs, until Louise's endless sobbing and self-pity got on her nerves so badly that she had to take what she believed to be serious and necessary action.

On her fourth afternoon at 45 Albert Square she strode into the front room, grabbed her sister by the shoulders and shook her violently.

'You've got to pull yourself together, girl!' she yelled in Louise's face. 'Anybody'd think there was a permanent ruddy wake goin' on in here!'

Louise stared like a sleepwalker who'd been slapped.

'What's the big tragedy, for God's sake? Albert's off doin' the same as thousands of other blokes, isn't he? Their old ladies are gettin' on with their lives, makin' the best of things. You're no different from them, even if you reckon you are.'

Louise tried to protest, but she hadn't the words.

'From here on, you can sink or swim.' Elsie gave her one more hard shake and released her. 'None of us is goin' to help you to stay like this.' With that Elsie stamped out into the hall and snatched her coat from the hook. 'I'm off!' she shouted. 'I'll come back and see you when you've got your head on straight!'

In spite of the shock tactics, it took several more days for Louise to rally. Perhaps shame or remorse finally worked the change – or, as she told herself later, maybe it was just time. She began to take stock of herself and gradually the credits started to encourage her; a nice house, sound little business, the dependence and love of four children who could lift her heart and fill the times when she missed Albert most. At the end of her deliberations Louise decided that, all in all, she was well-off.

She launched her return to the status of capable housewife with a thorough cleaning of the house, even though Elsie had left it spotless. She then set about a marathon session of washing and making repairs to the children's clothes. As the days passed she was amazed at how much better she felt – well enough, she decided, and certainly confident enough, to get back out among people and start working at the stall.

'I knew you'd snap out of it,' Elsie told her later. 'You're not the kind to buckle – not at bottom you ain't.'

They were in the Queen Victoria, the pub in Albert Square which had an entrance directly across the road from the yard exit of No 45. It was one o'clock and Louise had finished on the stall for the day; fruit was hard to come by and a lot of vegetables were scarce, but at least she always sold everything she had – nobody was in a position to pick and choose any more.

'I suppose you're right,' Louise said. 'I'm not exactly dancin' on air, but I'm a lot better in meself.' She smiled at her sister. 'There's hardly time to take stock of how I'm feelin' before it's time to go to bed and pass out. The days just fly.'

Elsie nodded and sipped her milk stout, a luxury now that controls on beer production had turned the pub into more of a meeting place than an ale house. 'The kids with Auntie Mave, are they?'

'Yes. Don't know what I'd do without her.' Mavis Elliot was the Beales' next-door neighbour, a hardy old widow who had known Louise's mother for thirty years. 'I saw her trottin' round the square at eleven o'clock, shovin' the pram with the other three strung out behind her.'

'What about the stall?'

'How d'you mean?'

'Albert said you was goin' to have to get somebody to help with wheeling it to an' from the lockup. Did you?'

Louise nodded over the rim of her glass. 'That chap from across the square. Reg Cox.'

'Cox.' Elsie searched her memory. 'What, you mean that one that's a soldier now?'

'That's right. Stationed at Woolwich, lucky beggar.'

'God yes, I know him,' Elsie said. 'His so-called missus left him two or three years back. The word was he thumped her a time or two when he'd been on the booze. What made you ask him?'

'I didn't have to ask – he offered.'

Although Elsie resembled Louise closely, she had a much wider range of facial expression. At that moment, she was wearing a look of darkest suspicion. 'Offered? From what I've heard, if that one was a ghost he wouldn't offer you a fright.'

'Well, that's as may be.' Louise sniffed. 'I speak as I find. He offered to move the barrow mornings and dinner times for me, so I said ta very much.'

'What about when he's not here?'

'He gets back quite a lot of the time, you'd be surprised. But when he's away he's arranged for his mate to do it for me.'

Elsie took a quarter of her drink to consider the situation. 'No,' she said finally, 'I wouldn't trust that one as far as I could throw a sheet of bum paper.'

'You've got an evil mind, Elsie.'

Elsie denied it with a shake of her head. 'I see things clear. Little kindnesses and a bit of flattery don't change my view of people.' She leaned close to Louise, lowering her voice. 'What's in it for him, eh?'

'Oh, for cryin' out loud – he's just helpin' out, that's all. He knows how I'm fixed, on me own with the kids an' a house to run as well as the stall . . .'

'He's not the charitable type,' Elsie insisted. 'Anyone'll tell you. If he has three pints with a mate he'll make sure the other bloke buys two of them.' Elsie waved to Gus, the landlord, as he came through from the other bar. 'We're just talking about that Cox bloke, Gus . . .'

'Yeah?' Gus came and leaned his thick forearms on the bar. 'What about him?'

'For any sake, Else,' Louise hissed. 'Stop makin' such a thing about it.'

Elsie ignored her. 'He's always been a bit tight, ain't he?'

'Well . . .' Gus frowned delicately. 'He *is* a customer here, from time to time, so I shouldn't really go talkin' about him – but yeah, you could call him tight. Mean, even.'

Elsie looked at the discomfited Louise. 'What did I tell you?'

'Never gives to collections,' Gus continued, his scant reticence about gossip now completely gone. 'Never buys anybody a drink unless he's sure of getting one back, preferably two.' He chuckled. 'The missus told me he always used to buy his bread just before the shop shut, when they'd knocked down the price to get rid of what was left.'

'Ever heard of him doin' anybody a favour?' Elsie asked.

Gus raised an eyebrow. 'Him? I've more chance of a love letter off Claudette Colbert than a good turn off Reg Cox.'

As Gus went into the other bar to serve a customer, Louise grabbed her sister's elbow, making her drink splash dangerously near the rim of the glass. 'What's your flamin' game, eh?' she demanded.

'I'm tryin' to let you see what kind of bloke it is that's bein' so *obligin'* all of a sudden.'

'You're stirrin' it, more like – makin' a fuss out of damn all!'

'Listen. I just don't think you should have anythin' to do with Cox. He don't help people, he never gives unless there's somethin' he wants back.'

'What do you mean by that?'

'You know exactly what I mean!'

'Elsie, you're still my little sister, even though you've been big with the advice lately. If you don't watch your mouth – '

'So what's Cox thinkin' to himself now?' Elsie's defensive note had become acid, taunting. 'What'll other people think? There you are, a young woman on her own, acceptin' this bloke's generosity like a flash the minute your old man's off to the army . . . What the hell's at the back of *your* mind, come to that?'

Louise stood up, slammed down her glass and strode out. She marched round to Mavis Elliot's, collected the children and took them home. When she had settled the baby for his nap and put Harry, Kenneth and Dora in the yard to play, she sat down at the kitchen table and clasped her hands to the sides of her head. She was still shaking.

'Bloody mare!' she growled at the wall.

She had been within an inch of hitting Elsie, which was as much a guide to the state of her nerves as a mark of her affront. It burned her to remember Elsie standing in this house, shaking her head and telling her to get herself sorted out; now, when she was doing just that – when she was taking steps to cope with a hard life the best way she could, the self-same Elsie was suddenly painting her as a flighty piece with rickety morals and no concern for her reputation.

'Mum.' Dora was standing by the open door with one hand clasped around the other, one small finger standing up stiffly. There was a trickle of blood from the knuckle.

'Oh, love . . .' Louise went to her and picked her up. 'What have you been doin' to yourself now?'

'A brick did it.'

Louise kissed the finger as she carried the child to the sink. 'Rotten old brick, goin' for you like that. I'll take a stick to it after.'

Dora watched solemnly as her mother ran water on to the scratch. 'I didn't cry or nothin',' she pointed out.

'Didn't you want to?'

'A bit. But Auntie Elsie says cryin's soppy.'

Louise gazed at the serious little face. 'It's not always soppy,' she said. 'Sometimes you've just got to cry, 'cause you can't help it. It boils over.' She dabbed the finger dry and stood Dora by the table while she got the Germolene from the cupboard.

'Is it soppy when you cry too much?'

'I suppose so.'

'Were you bein' soppy?'

Louise came back with the ointment. 'Maybe I was, love.' She patted the four-year-old head. 'But I promise I won't be soppy again.'

Later sitting at the kitchen table and reading again the three brief letters she'd had from Albert, Louise began to see herself from the children's point of view. They had been so good the past couple of weeks, yet for most of the time they must have been bewildered. Their dad had gone and their mum did nothing but bubble and mope. It pained her to realize that just when she should have been giving them extra attention, she had all but rejected them. That, she decided firmly, would never happen to them again.

'No more soppiness,' she whispered, smiling as she folded the letters.

She got up and put on the kettle. As she waited for it to boil, her mind jolted back to the painful exchange with her sister. That was something else she had to take in hand. Elsie needed shoving into line.

From the yard the five-year-old, Harry, called to her. 'Can we all go for a walk, Mum?'

'I'll think about it, love.'

She held on to the interrupted thought. It had been a mistake, she realized, to let Elsie into the house and run things, even for an hour. It had been wrong to let *anyone* see her defeated and self-pitying. She understood, instinctively and sharply, that even with the best intentions, people abuse what they know to be vulnerable; Elsie had had the effrontery to decry her behaviour and moralize at her – something she had never dared do before.

Feeling a new determination swell in her, Louise decided that in her mother's house she would become the respected figure that old woman had been. The strength was in her, she only had to do herself some justice by bringing it forward.

'And that young cow Elsie better watch out,' she murmured.

As the kettle started to boil Harry's grubby face poked through the doorway. 'Mum . . .'

'I've made up me mind,' Louise told him. 'We'll go for a walk, just as soon as I've had a cuppa.' She watched his features brighten.

'Can we maybe get some toffees?'

Louise pretended to think about it, then nodded. 'If there's toffees to be had anywhere in Walford, you'll all get some.'

'Honest?'

'Honest.' She wrinkled her nose at him. 'I'm your mum, right? I'm here to look after you. If I promise you something, then you'll get it.'

Harry went off to tell the other two. Louise began to hum brightly as she poured steaming water into the teapot.

4

'Odd, that fellow Hess coming here,' Gregory Legg observed. He speared a piece of cod with his fork and nibbled at it. 'At first they thought he'd run away, then there was some story about him being sent to talk terms with the King, of all people. Now I hear he might possibly be a lunatic.'

Harold had finished eating. He watched his sister, Miriam, as she prepared to comment on what their father had said. She was always doing that, Harold thought; nothing ever seemed to spring to her lips casually, it had to be shaped, rehearsed in her head, then issued like an official bulletin.

'He's Deputy Führer,' she said at last, 'and Leader of the NSDAP. I would say he's far from being a lunatic, and he's much too important to Hitler to be offered up as a hostage.'

Her father nodded. 'So what's he doing here?'

'Furthering the cause, perhaps.' Miriam was only twenty-two, but she had the speech and mannerisms of a much older woman. In many ways she reminded Harold of a female Mike Phillips. 'It doesn't stretch credibility too far, does it, to suppose he might be here at the invitation of certain anti-Semitic elements in Britain.'

Harold stared at her. 'That's ridiculous,' he said.

Miriam glared. 'It was only because his plane came down that anyone knew he was here. For all we know he was heading for a secret rendezvous.'

Her father had begun eating more earnestly, which

meant he didn't want to pursue the discussion in the direction Miriam had turned it.

'And what would he be doing at this secret destination?' Harold demanded.

Miriam chewed slowly, preparing another statement. 'Who knows? But if the second loftiest Nazi in the world is here, it has to be something very big, and very ugly.' She paused and leaned forward for emphasis. 'Their chief priority is the extermination of the Jewish people. There are plenty of powerful men in this country who wouldn't be averse to aiding and abetting that scheme. Bargains could be struck at the expense of a few thousand lives.'

Harold blinked. 'That's downright paranoid, Miriam.'

'I'd expect a remark like that from you.'

'The same as I expect all the baloney you're always coming out with.'

'Now, now,' their father warned. 'Let's not have any squabbling at the dinner table.'

The door opened and Mrs Legg entered the dining room. She was a short, pneumatic woman with multiple chins, sorrowful eyes and voluminous grey hair, worn high to give her stature.

'Another committee problem?' her husband asked as she sat down at the table. She had been on the telephone for five minutes.

'It was a man from the local paper. He wanted details of our fund-raising scheme.' As she picked up her fork she noticed the scowl on Miriam's broad face. 'What's the matter?'

Miriam jerked her head at Harold. 'Him. Every time I open my mouth he sneers.'

'I wasn't sneering. I was just making the observation that you're obsessed. Which you are.'

Mrs Legg didn't need to know any more. She looked at Harold. 'What kind of doctor will you make,' she asked coldly, 'if you habitually disregard people's feelings and principles?'

'Not disregarding, mother,' he said sharply. 'Analysing – the way a good doctor should.'

'Harold!' His father snapped.

'What have I said that's wrong?' Harold slammed down his knife. 'If I make one comment about Miriam's rabid Judaism I'm automatically a villain – but she can come out with as much wrong-headed, bigoted tommy-rot as she likes and get a pat on the back for it.'

Mrs Legg replaced her fork on the plate and folded her hands. It was a signal that she was going into one of her hurt silences.

Harold stood up. 'Excuse me.' He went out, closing the door firmly behind him. As Gregory went on eating and the two women exchanged despairing shakes of the head, the front door slammed.

It was only a short walk to his uncle's place. As always, Leon was delighted to see Harold. 'Your timing is impeccable,' he said, leading him into the tiny sitting room.

'Why's that?'

'*Das Lied Von Der Erde*,' Leon said. 'A friend loaned me the recordings. I was just about to sit down with a sherry and listen to them.'

'Marvellous. I love Mahler.' Harold unbuttoned his jacket and sat down on the misshapen old couch. 'I see you've got a new picture.'

Leon nodded at the plain wooden frame over the fireplace. 'It's a Turner – Hero and Leander. Picked it up for sixpence in a junk shop.'

Harold nodded approvingly, running his eyes along all the familiar prints and ornaments, the ancient furniture. Since childhood he had adored this room. It was always welcoming and cosy, complementing Uncle Leon himself, an appealingly untidy man who had always radiated warmth and kindness. One of the records was already revolving on the turntable of the cabinet gramophone – his uncle's only luxury.

'I'm afraid the sherry's a bit ordinary,' Leon muttered, bringing a glass. 'But maybe the music will do something for it.'

'I'm sure it will.'

'Now, then . . .' Leon went to the gramophone. He moved the arm across and lowered the needle into the groove. There was some crackling, then the opening bars welled from the speaker. Leon toasted Harold silently, sipped his sherry and sat down.

Harold closed his eyes as the pure clarity of a human voice joined the splendour of the orchestra. This was his ideal of peace, to sit comfortably and be bathed by beautiful music; this room was the only place outside of a concert hall or recital room where he could enjoy it. His mother found music irritating after only a few minutes – a fact which said a lot about her personal disharmony – so he rarely played any at home. It was always to Leon's he came for this special pleasure, and just as often for companionship and advice.

Harold opened his eyes and smiled at the rapturous expression on his uncle's face. Leon was a professional musician, a second violinist with the Queen's Hall Orchestra. In Harold's family's view he was a failure. He was paid badly and the work was erratic; to make ends meet, he had to do extra sessions at the Lyons Corner House Brasserie. But Harold didn't think Leon was a failure. He was doing what he wanted to do, after all. And he was happy.

Too soon the music was over. Leon closed the gramophone lid, refilled the sherry glasses and drew his chair closer to the couch. 'So,' he said, settling himself. 'How are things?'

'At Bart's, things are going well,' Harold said. 'It's hectic, mind you, but what else can I expect? I'm making progress.'

'And at home?'

'No change. I'm never comfortable there any more. I think maybe it's time for me to make a move.'

'That bad?'

Harold nodded. 'There's always some row or other breaking out. I'm sure a lot of it's my fault, but Miriam and my mother . . .' He shrugged. 'They're hard to live with.'

Leon rubbed his nose thoughtfully. 'Holy zeal's always tough company,' he murmured.

'They seem to think I'm making fun of them, or mocking their ideals. But I'm not – I just can't see that being Jewish means you've got to be . . .' He paused, trying to find words to explain what he meant.

'Eternally proclaiming the faith,' Leon said.

'Right. I've told them how I feel about it. I don't want to belong to any sect, religion or country for that matter. I don't know how many times I've made it clear, but it's only these past few months they've given up trying to get me round to their way of thinking.'

Harold had talked about the matter to Leon before. 'Well, if they've stopped trying, you must be making some kind of headway.'

Harold's father had changed their name to Legg, after the street they lived in, when the East End jews began attracting hostile attention. Harold's personal experience of persecution had been sobering, even frightening; he had witnessed Mosley whipping up anti-Jewish hatred at his meetings, he had seen the Fascist marches in the East

End. At school he was often referred to as 'Jew-boy' and once or twice he was beaten.

But he had witnessed other bigotries – Catholic versus Protestant, heterosexuals victimizing homosexuals, rich persecuting poor – and he had decided that sects, factions, nationalism, strict political ideologies and religions were profoundly bad for humanity.

'A pox on all their houses,' Uncle Leon had remarked more than once when the topic was raised. Nevertheless, Harold had been obliged to live with a mother and sister whose rigid Jewish faith both underlined his conviction and, at times, drove him close to distraction.

'I don't know how my father puts up with it,' he told Leon.

'He doesn't. He lives beyond it.'

On reflection, Harold realized that was true. His father, in no way an orthodox Jew, simply remained separate from the women's Judaism. He seemed to be capable of switching off his reactions, and he never ventured a comment, for or against.

'I wish I could be like him, in that respect,' Harold said. 'But I can't let them get away with some of the things they say and do – not without some kind of protest.'

'Somebody once said that all the truth in the world can be condensed into a single sentence,' Leon said. 'The sentence is, "And this too shall pass away." All things change, Harold, you'll be out on your own one day. In the meantime, if you want an old rogue's advice, find some strong distraction. A nice young woman, for example.'

Harold smiled ruefully. 'The only one that's seriously taken my fancy turns out to be going steady with somebody else.'

'Have you tried to show her the error of her ways?'

'Of course not. I don't approve of poaching.'

Leon chuckled. 'Harold, that kind of morality can be the death of your social life. You're looking at it all wrong, anyway.'

'Why do you say that?'

Leon rested his elbows on his knees and clasped his hands, as he usually did when he handed out advice. 'For all you know, the girl is going steady with this fellow because she's been offered no alternative. In my long and reprehensible experience, that's very often been the case. She's pretty young, I assume?'

'Nineteen.'

'The younger they are, the more likely it is that their constancy is the result of no other offers being put forward.'

'You think so?'

'I know whereof I speak, Harold,' Leon said, a trifle indignantly. 'And here's something else to bear in mind. If you ask her to go out with you there's a chance she'll accept, and something may develop. Leave things as they are and there's no chance of that at all.'

Harold was suddenly enthusiastic. It was a month since he had met and spoken to Judith Martin; he hadn't seen her since, but she lingered in his mind like a sweet, soft pain.

'I, erm, I'm not very experienced at asking girls out, actually . . .'

'Good. That means you haven't got a line of patter that's gone lifeless with wear. You'll think of something, Harold, don't worry. Let inspiration take care of you.'

Later, as he was leaving, Harold paused on the door-step and grinned at his uncle. 'Not a bad evening, all things considered,' he said. 'Thanks for the recital and the advice to the lovelorn.'

'Don't come back here until you've spoken to the girl,' Leon warned him. 'If you do, I won't let you in.'

They embraced warmly, then Harold hurried off down the path.

Next morning he was at St Bartholomew's before nine. For much of a restless night he had rehearsed what he would do, how he would do it, even how he would look. He had on his best suit and an uncomfortable but highly fashionable pair of brogues. He had put some Brylcreem on his hair and had even considered clipping his eyebrows, until he recalled reading that some women found dark, thick eyebrows attractive.

His first call was at Emergency, which was relatively quiet. He made a thorough search of the place, but didn't locate Nurse Martin. When he asked a Sister where she might be, he was informed icily that it was no business of his, since he wasn't technically on the staff – and besides, she didn't recall the name.

At Men's Medical he had to pretend to be waiting to see the Consultant, just to get himself inside the ward. Again, he drew a blank. There was no sign of Nurse Martin and the duty roster was in the Sister's office.

On his way across to Women's Medical he tried not to contemplate defeat. The iron was hot, he'd been all night heating it, and if he didn't strike today – this very morning – his courage might desert him. But what if she was off on leave, or sick, or had been transferred? Perhaps she'd even gone to another hospital – that kind of thing was happening all the time.

He closed his mind to foreboding, reminding himself firmly that to think positively was to achieve. Just inside the entrance to the ward he paused, wondering how to get a look at the nurses. He had a feeling that the waiting-to-see-the-Consultant ploy wouldn't work again; it had barely worked the first time. While he was standing there a Staff Nurse saw him from the office and came across.

'Can I help you?'

'I – I'm waiting for someone . . .'

'Are you a visitor?' The woman had hard, suspicious eyes. Harold supposed he looked pretty suspicious skulking there, shifting from foot to foot. 'Visiting hours are printed clearly outside the gate.'

'No, I'm not visiting.' Harold glanced beyond her shoulder, trying to see inside.

'Then you mustn't loiter here.'

'I'm a medical student. I just wanted – '

'I'm sorry. No students are permitted in the ward unless they have an appointment with Sister, or are accompanied by senior medical staff.'

Harold had the feeling that any second now she might raise the alarm. 'Look, I just wanted to pass on a message to a nurse . . .'

Now the hard eyes narrowed. 'A personal message?'

He nodded. 'Personal and private, Staff. If you wouldn't mind letting me see the young woman in person for a moment, if she's here that is – '

'Leave.'

'I'm sure you're misunderstanding all this – '

'I said leave. If you don't I'll call the security office.'

Harold backed out into the corridor. The Staff Nurse stood and watched him as he wandered off in the direction of the lecture block.

'That's that,' he sighed. So much for thinking positively. He would have had more chance in a convent, the way security and suspicion joined hands in this place. He looked at his watch. He had a lecture in three minutes. He began to walk more briskly, knowing the little cloud of disappointment would grow to a blanket of depression as the day wore on. That was what happened when Lewis had told him Judith was going steady.

As he approached the anatomy lecture theatre, he began to wonder if he hadn't, after all, had a lucky escape. The plan, viewed in the increasingly cold light of failure, looked a bit crazy. He wasn't the kind of swashbuckler to try something like that. What would she have thought of him if he'd carried it through? Pushy, that's what. Presumptuous. A pest. Whatever she thought, she would have turned him down flat, because he would have made a mess of it. The technique might work for the likes of Uncle Leon, but was it really the thing for someone of Harold's age and inexperience to attempt?

He paused by the lecture room door, hearing a droning, authoritarian voice from within. He looked at his watch again, then at the corridor clock.

'Oh, God, no . . .'

His watch was four minutes slow. The lecture had started. Now, to top the morning's rich tide of stress he would have to interrupt, apologize and probably be black-marked. He took a deep breath and reached for the door knob.

'Good morning, Mr Legg.'

He turned, blinked once and felt his heart thud violently on his ribs. It was her. She was right there, in front of him, *smiling at him*, looking impossibly beautiful in her red and blue cape.

'Oh, hello there.' He moistened his lips, scared she would move off again before he could say anything. 'Going on duty, are you?'

'Off. I'm on nights for a month.'

He nodded, rather too vigorously he felt, wondering what to say next. His heart surged again as she made to move on. 'I say . . .'

She paused, smiling, eyes politely questioning.

He heard himself speak without knowing how he had summoned the words. 'I wondered if you might like to go out one evening. Spot of dinner, something like that.' He was appalled at how oily he sounded. His mind cringed, ready for the rejection.

'That would be nice.'

'Mm? Oh.' He was stunned.

'I'm not on duty Friday night, if that would suit you.'

Now adrenalin surged. 'That would be perfect,' he said. 'Shall I meet you somewhere – home, perhaps? You're in Fulham, aren't you?'

She gave him the address and he wrote it in his notebook.

'Eight o'clock be all right?'

She nodded. 'I'll look forward to it. By the way, my name's Judith.'

'I know.' He watched her smile and felt his knees dissolving. 'I'm Harold.'

'I'll see you on Friday then, Harold.' She smiled again, waved and clopped away in her little black shoes.

He was inside the lecture theatre before he knew it, dazed, delirious, too happy to be in control of himself. He saw the lecturer staring at him. Then he realized everybody was staring. The place was terribly quiet.

'Sorry I'm late, sir,' he said. 'I got held up.'

'Just sit down then, Legg, and we can proceed.'

He dropped into a chair as the others returned their attention to the lectern. One person, he noticed, was still staring. It was Phillips, frowning as he always did at anyone less punctual than himself. His expression changed sharply as Harold smiled broadly at him and winked.

5

In July Albert Beale wrote to say that he would not, after all, be having embarkation leave. It was a brief, bleak letter that mirrored his dejection and his misgivings about what lay ahead. He could not say where he was going; all he could tell his wife was that he was now officially a trained soldier of the Middlesex Regiment, and they were going overseas. He would write as often as he could.

Louise's strict policy, now, was that she would rise above any disappointment and give in to no setback, however much it bruised her. But that night, after she had read the letter over and over, drawing every drop of meaning and affection from the stilted words, she cried herself to sleep.

Life went on, nevertheless. The disappointment of Albert's cancelled leave soon merged with all the other unrelenting hardships of her daily life – poor trade, rationing, restrictions, shortages and – lately – illnesses among the children.

Ronnie was eleven months old and Kenneth was three; at the end of June they had simultaneously contracted measles. They were not fully recovered when Harry caught a pulmonary virus and became so ill he had to be nursed night and day for over a week. At the end of his illness he had lost three pounds in weight. Louise, who had refused all but a minimum of help from her sisters, was lighter by half a stone.

On a warm, bright evening a few days after Harry had passed the crisis of his illness, Mavis Elliot came in from next door and virtually ordered Louise out of the house.

'I've been sittin' round there thinkin' what a time of it you've had lately,' Mavis said. 'And you've been shut up in here every night since your Albert went away.' She shook her head and tutted with the special authority conferred by age. 'You must feel like you're in gaol. Go on out and get yourself some fresh air. I'll see to the nippers.'

The notion of a little time on her own was tempting. There were benches in the small garden in the middle of the square, and already that evening Louise had looked out and thought how nice it would be just to sit there for a while.

'Are you sure, Auntie Mave? I mean the kids are a bit of a handful just now, cranky an' that . . .'

'On you go out of it. I like them pesterin' me. Makes me feel needed.'

'Right then. I'll just have half an hour or so.'

Louise was surprised how warm it was outside; she could have done without the cardigan she was wearing. She stood by the gate, inhaling the gentle breeze, feeling rather light-headed as she gazed around the Victorian square.

A memory surfaced. A year ago, she had stood on that spot with her mother, conscious of the foreshadowing frailty in the old lady. Louise had wanted to sit in the garden then too, but her mother had felt cold, even though it had been a close, airless evening. She had fallen ill the next day and had never set foot outside again.

For a moment Louise was held by a sharp, renewed pining for her mother's sheltering presence. At her bidding it passed quickly, as all her sadness did nowadays, fading to a poignant echo as she walked across the road and into the garden.

She sat on a warm bench among small trees and bushes, catching their fragrance as she watched the feathery shadows of leaves and branches on the ground. On an impulse she decided she would try to describe this in her next letter to Albert – just the act of sitting here, feeling the late sun, looking about her. It would do him good, stuck in whatever foreign hole they'd put him, to get a reminder of the Square, of summer in London.

'Makes you feel good to be alive, weather like this,' a man's voice said. She turned and saw Reg Cox; he had come into the garden by the gate opposite his front door. He was in uniform and carrying an important-looking attache case. 'I was just goin' into the house when I spotted you here.' He came across and sat down beside her. 'Smashin' night, eh?'

'Lovely,' Louise agreed. Ever since the tirade from Elsie, she had felt awkward in Reg's presence – almost as if by talking to him she was giving life to the black innuendos her sister had dropped.

Reg set the case carefully on his knees and smiled at her. He had a crooked smile that uncovered yellowy tombstone teeth. 'How are the kids now?'

'Oh, a lot better. They're well past the worst.'

'That's good. Any word from your husband?'

Louise told him about Albert's leave being cancelled.

'Oh dear.' Reg shook his head sadly. 'That's a shame. Makes the likes of me feel a bit guilty, being posted so near home, gettin' home all the time . . .'

'Luck of the draw,' Louise said, to make him feel better about it.

'I suppose you're right. But it is a pain all the same, Lou – you don't mind me calling you Lou, do you?'

'No, 'course I don't.' It had always been Mrs Beale before, but Louise truly didn't mind the familiarity; she was Lou to practically everybody she knew. And he had asked if it was all right, unlike a few traders, suppliers and the like who'd used her first name even before she knew who they were.

'Tell you what,' Reg said. He undid the catch on the case and slipped his hand inside. Although the lid was raised only a fraction and for just a moment before he withdrew his hand again, Louise saw that it was crammed with boxes and packets. Reg dropped four bars of Fry's Sandwich chocolate in her lap. 'Present for the kids.'

'Oh, no, really I couldn't . . .'

'Yes you can, an' I'm not havin' them back. Hide them away in the pocket of your woolly, mind. Don't want folk seein'.'

'It's really very good of you. The kids'll be thinkin' it's Christmas.' Louise scooped up the bars and pocketed them. Some miser, she thought.

Reg set the bag carefully at his feet. 'My mate George been lookin' after you all right while I've been away? Gettin' the old barrow out on time an' that?'

Louise nodded. 'Regular and on the dot.'

'Good. You remember, now, any other help you need, humpin' or carryin', just say the word. Always glad to give a hand. It can't be easy for you, tacklin' all that on your own.'

The man's generosity, considering she had known him less than two months, was dazzling. It would certainly have raised a suspicion or two in Louise – with or without his reputation of being mean – if it weren't for the fact that he'd played the perfect gentleman all along.

'Cigarette?' he offered.

'No thanks.'

'You don't mind me havin' a puff, do you? I know it bothers some folk, smoke blowin' in their faces.'

'No, no, you go right ahead.'

There it was again, Louise thought, a refreshing bit of gentlemanly consideration. Right from the start, when he'd politely offered to move the barrow back and forth, there had been no sign, whatever, of a tendency to take liberties.

Louise had thought it over carefully, after the row with Elsie. She had come to a straightforward conclusion. Reg Cox was a careful man, that was all. He didn't throw his money about. In some people's eyes that was being mean. In Louise's experience, he was a helpful, generous, courteous person, and that was that. As for the business with his wife – or whatever she was – that was more than likely another one of the nasty rumours people were always concocting when they didn't know the facts.

'The chocolate, by the way,' Reg said, 'it isn't illegal or nothing.'

'I'm sure it isn't.'

'Just one of the perks of the job.' He looked at his watch. 'It's a grand night for sittin' about in the open, but I've got to get a move on.' He stood up. 'Nice to see you, anyway.' He smiled and touched his forage cap. 'Keep well, now.'

As he picked up the case and walked off Louise thanked him again for the chocolate. Moments later, when she heard his front door click shut, she slipped her hand into her cardigan pocket and broke a square off one of the bars. Just one piece, she promised, then popped it into her mouth.

During August Louise was forced to make a decision that she would sooner have left to Albert. The fruit and vegetable stall, apart from taking up time that she could scarcely spare, had been bringing in less and less money throughout the summer. There were few apples and no bananas to be found any more. No onions either. Lemons were so scarce that they were auctioned for charity. Oranges were reserved for children and they were only supplied to certain shops. The quality of green vegetables had diminished and so had the quantities that were available. There were plenty of carrots, parsnips and turnips, but people were sick of them.

'I can't run a business floggin' just potatoes, can I?' Louise had complained to one of her suppliers at the end of July.

Not long after, a propaganda character called Potato Pete started to appear in the papers and on posters, encouraging people to eat more potatoes than bread. Mr Carrot was the next one to arrive, telling the population how even cakes could be improved by the inclusion of carrots instead of other ingredients. Both characters, apart from proclaiming their nutritional benefits, pointed out that it was unpatriotic not to favour them over other foods.

From then on it was clear, Louise decided, that her stall would be the last one anyone would want to patronize, now that the Government was trying to blackmail the public into buying her stock. As the days passed, business did fall off even more than before. In the third week of August Louise stopped trading.

It was an overnight decision, though it had been on the cards long enough. There was regret among the other stall holders when they heard. Beale's Fruit and Veg had been part of the street market for many years, always occupying the same position outside the Queen Victoria. It was the last stall along the tail-end stretch of barrows that ran from the rail bridge to the pub on the corner of Bridge Street and Albert Square. It had been passed on to Albert Beale by his Aunt Dolly, a spinster who brought him up after both his parents died of influenza in the 1919 epidemic.

On the same morning she announced she was going out of business, there was an impromptu party for Louise in the Queen Victoria. Traders minded each others' stalls as they came along in pairs to have a swift half of watery beer and wish her all the best.

Jimmy Douglas, who ran the wet fish stall under the bridge, said it just wasn't going to be the same on the market without Louise. 'I'm goin' to miss that sweet soprano voice bellowin' out the prices all mornin' long.'

'I shan't miss it,' Betty Greaves said, winking. She had the pie and mash shop next door to the pub. 'Fair rattles me windows, sometimes. When she was in really good voice, I had to hand out ear plugs to the customers.'

Louise had consumed three milk stouts and was feeling more emotional than she would normally permit. The stall had become nothing but a pain to her, a time and energy waster. But now it had come to the moment of abandoning the venture she was full of regret. She sat on the warm leather of a corner seat with sunlight from the etched windows gilding her head and shoulders; she felt more like a minor sovereign at an abdication ceremony. No more fruit and vegetables on the market. It was the closing of an era.

'It ain't for good,' she assured everyone. 'I'll open up again when things ease. If they ever do.'

'Have you thought of changin' to somethin' else?' somebody asked. 'There's still all kinds of gear to be had. If you put your mind to it and look around the suppliers.'

Louise shook her head firmly. 'Beale's has always been fruit an' veg. It always will be. Each to his own trade.'

'It's going to be hard,' the landlord's wife, Flo, pointed out, 'just living on what the army gives you.'

'I'll manage.'

'With family, friends an' neighbours, you'll always get by,' Jimmy Douglas said. He stepped forward from the bar and put a parting gift on the table in front of Louise. 'Nice bit of cod for your tea,' he murmured. 'Oh, and I want you to have this, too.' He picked up a small board that had been leaning against the bar. 'You always said it tickled you, and I don't find a lot of use for it these days.'

Louise took the board and smiled at it. In 1940, when supplies of fish had begun to fluctuate wildly, Jimmy had always put the sign on his stall whenever stocks were good:

PLENTY OF HERRING
ALL OVER THE PLAICE.
DON'T TELL A SOLE!

'I'll get it framed,' Louise said. She looked up at the smiling faces around her. She lived just across the way, but it felt like a real parting. She wouldn't be one of them any more. 'You've all been good to me. The best mates a girl could have.' Another milk stout appeared on the table beside her. She picked up the glass and moved it in a slow arc from left to right. 'Bless you all.'

At a quarter to twelve, after more toasts and well-wishing, Louise stepped out on to the street and looked at her empty barrow. It had been put there early, before she'd had time to tell Reg Cox there would be no need for it. She sighed. The old thing looked pathetic, standing there in its bare-board redundancy. She would lock it away herself, she decided. When the war was over and they could trade again, she would be the first to wheel it out again.

Reg Cox looked troubled when she asked him for the key to the lock-up. He stood in his doorway frowning, rubbing his chin.

'I've gone an' left the key with George – I didn't think I'd be here dinner time.' He shook his head. 'Lord knows where he is. Tell you what, just leave the barrow standing there, Lou. He'll like as not take it away as soon as he shows up, then I'll get the key back to you.'

Louise explained, rather awkwardly, that she wanted to put the barrow away herself. 'Just a bit of sentimentality,' she added.

Reg frowned. 'Oh. In that case I'll scout around and find George. I'll bring the key to you as soon as I can.'

Louise thanked him for his trouble and went back across the square to the house. She stepped into the yard and inspected the few boxes that were piled there. Since the time they were married, it had been Albert's practice to keep his supplies at her mother's house, some stacked in the yard and some in the hallway. It meant the heavy barrow could always be moved empty to and from the lock-up; the stock had only to be carried a few steps from the yard to their pitch outside the pub. The arrangement had been made with gran's approval, on the understanding that she could always help herself to whatever she needed.

'Changed days,' Louise murmured, recalling how bulging, close-stacked crates used to top the wall. She had a swift rummage. Apart from a few pounds of potatoes, some limp-leaved cabbages and a box of carrots, there was nothing left worth keeping. She decided she would divide the stuff among the family, then clear the boxes from the yard so the children would have more room to play.

To make a start she piled up some slatted wooden display trays and took them across to the fish stall; Jimmy Douglas could find a use for just about anything. On the way back she glanced across the square and saw Reg Cox leaning in through the window of his mate George's little black van. They were talking earnestly. As Louise watched, Reg got into the van and it drove off.

At three o'clock she began to wonder what was wrong. Her barrow was the only one left on Bridge Street, looking more forlorn than ever. George still hadn't appeared with the key.

At half-past three she went and knocked on Reg Cox's door. There was no reply. She stood in the square and looked about her, bewildered. In all the time they'd had their arrangement, Reg Cox had never once turned up late; neither had George. Now, on the very day she packed in the business, there was no sign of either of them.

At four o'clock, after hunting through bags and boxes and finally locating an old, rusty spare key to the lock-up, Louise started trundling the barrow towards the railway bridge. It was a three-minute walk to the lock-up, an old, isolated brick structure that had been built into the railway embankment over sixty years before. It had once been used as a lamp store, but it had fallen into disuse until Albert's aunt bought it from the railway authorities, for a few nominal shillings, in 1920.

The barrow seemed to get heavier as Louise rounded the corner, dragging it behind her, imagining fancifully that it didn't want to be put away. Panting, she straightened the wheels and made an effort to get up some momentum. The effort kept her bent forward, her eyes on the road, arms straining until the wheels began to turn more easily on the level stretch of road.

A hundred yards from the lock-up she suddenly leaned back on the swivelled handle, trying to stop the barrow. Frantically she twisted the wheels to the left, making friction with the kerb finally bring them to a halt.

Gasping for breath, she stood staring towards the lock-up. The door was half open, and the little black van was standing outside.

Keeping close to the embankment, Louise moved up to the door and listened. There was the sound of something heavy being dragged across the cement floor, then she heard Reg Cox's voice.

'Two more trips, if this lot'll fit.'

'Three. I'll put money on it.' his mate George grunted. 'What a buggerin' turn up this is.'

'You've said that about twenty times. It don't help. I got us someplace else, didn't I? That's all that matters.'

'Not as good as this,' George moaned, pushing the door wider as he backed out.

'Best I could do in an emergency.'

Louise grasped the edge of the door and drew it wide open. The two men were sliding a loaded tea chest between them. Reg Cox saw her at once. George took a moment to react. He caught Reg's expression, glanced over his shoulder, then straightened.

'What the hell's all this?' Louise stared at the rows of stacked boxes with Government markings, the piles of folded blankets, crates of spirit bottles and dozens of multi-coloured confectionery cartons.

'Ah, hello, Lou.' Reg tried to grin, but it looked more like he was going to be sick. George glared at her.

'Well?' she demanded.

'A few things we took the liberty of storin',' Reg said, 'since there's the room here, and we didn't have anywhere else. I knew you wouldn't mind. We're movin' the stuff out now . . .'

Nearly every day Louise read reports in the papers about WD and Red Cross supplies being stolen, about bonded spirits disappearing and wholesalers' stocks of confectionery, tinned food and cigarettes mysteriously shrinking. It was happening on an epidemic scale, the *Daily Mirror* had reported, and the goods were regularly finding their way on to the black market.

'Looks like Aladdin's cave to me,' she snapped. 'More perks, is it?'

Reg was about to say something when George cut in.

'Just you forget what you've seen, right? It's unhealthy stickin' your nose in.'

Righteous anger gripped Louise. 'Don't you dare threaten me!' she shouted, making George take a step back. 'One word in the right ear an' I can have you hammered flat *before* you're handed over to the law!'

She switched her attention to Reg. 'You've been playin' me for a mug, haven't you?'

'Now then, Lou . . .'

'Nice little hidey-hole, this. Just the place to stack your contraband. An' if the police had found out I'd be right in the muck.'

'No, no,' Reg objected, making a placating gesture with his hand. 'Nothing like that . . .'

'Don't come it, you crooked bugger! How long have you had the key to this place? Near enough three months, isn't it? Three months usin' my premises for somethin' that could get me a couple of years in Holloway.' She felt like hitting him. She felt like hitting herself for being taken in so easily.

'Look . . .' Reg spread his hands helplessly; 'Suppose we make you a present of some of this, then we just forget the whole thing, eh?'

'Sod off!'

Reg frowned apprehensively. 'What are you goin' to do?'

'She can't do nothin'!' George barked. 'Who'd believe she wasn't in on it?'

Louise felt herself turn white. It was in her to claw the eyes out of them both. 'I'll tell you what I'm goin' to do,' she said, her voice unnervingly quiet. 'I'm goin' to go home. When you've got rid of this lot, you'll find my barrow down the road there. Lock it away and drop the key through my letterbox.'

Relief began to spread on Reg's face. 'You're not goin' to spout on us?'

'I hadn't finished,' Louise said. 'When you've delivered the key back to me, you go into the Queen Vic and give Gus fifty quid for the Red Cross box. Tell him you collected it, if you like.'

Reg gaped. '*Fifty*?'

'You can go to hell,' George snapped.

'Hell won't have a look-in if you don't do it. There's still some very handy lads about Walford. They ain't all in the army yet – an' a lot of them would be glad to do Albert Beale's missus a favour.'

'Look, Lou, what if we just – '

'If you argue,' she warned Reg, 'the price of your neck goes up to a hundred.'

For a moment they were silent, motionless, Reg staring at Louise, reading the sincerity of her threat, George staring dully at Reg. Finally Reg nodded. 'Right you are,' he murmured.

'An' see you pay up tonight.'

'I will.'

Louise looked at them for another second, then turned sharply and walked away. For a long time after she got home she stood in the kitchen, castigating herself for being so stupid, so gullible. If Elsie ever found out she would have a field day, gloating, rubbing it in. Louise didn't even dare imagine what Albert's reaction would be. Neither of them would find out, though. Nobody at all would. Louise would hang on to the knowledge. It would be a memory to roast herself with whenever she ran the risk of letting somebody take advantage of her again.

While she was still standing there Mavis Elliot tapped the door and came in. She was carrying young Ronnie. He was fast asleep, his head resting on her shoulder.

'The other three are playing in my yard,' she said. 'They're happy enough for now. I thought this one had better have his nap in his pram.'

'Thanks, Auntie Mave.' Louise took the baby gently and put him in his pram in the hallway. When she came back she nodded at the teapot. 'Cuppa?'

'Love one.' As Louise filled the kettle Mavis frowned at her. 'You all right, love? You were lookin' a bit strange when I came in.'

'Oh, I was just frettin' about things.' She put the kettle on the cooker and lit the gas. 'Thinkin' how much there is to learn when you don't have your old man about the place.'

'It won't be forever, love.'

Louise nodded. 'I know. An' I know somethin' else. I'll be a lot sharper by the time my Albert gets back. You see if I'm not.'

6

'Mr Phillips,' the neurology lecturer said, 'perhaps you could tell us how you would conduct a routine examination of a patient's nervous system.'

It was the beginning of the second week in February, 1942, the first day of term following a longer-than-usual winter break enforced by staff shortages. The students, in the lecturer's stated view, had become slack from their long idleness. He had been giving them a rough morning.

'Make your points clearly, if you will. I'm growing tired of fuddled delivery.'

Phillips stood up, pushing back a strand of lank hair. He hadn't been prepared for the question, since he had already volunteered an observation on spinal movement and didn't think he would be asked to contribute anything else. 'Well.' He stared at the ceiling for a moment. 'Starting with the gait – '

'No, Mr Phillips,' the lecturer said irritably. 'You do not start with the gait. First you would check the subject's mental state.'

'Sorry, sir.'

'So you should be. We went over this many times towards the end of last term.'

'Yes. Sorry.'

'You've already apologized. Proceed.'

Phillips took a deep breath. 'I'd check the function of the cranial nerves.'

'No. You're charging ahead again.'

Phillips blushed and glared at another student who was grinning. As a young man who traded constantly in facts, mostly disjointed and unrelated, he had trouble fitting logical steps in the right order. He gave the lecturer a pained look. 'The history?' he ventured in a small voice.

'Yes, the history. What would you find in the taking of a history that might give an indication of a man or woman's mental state?'

It had been a wild guess. Phillips stared blankly at the lecturer.

'Oh, sit down. Legg, can you do any better?'

Phillips slumped into his seat and glowered at Harold, who had stood up at once.

'There's no need to ask specific questions to determine mental state,' he said, trying not to sound too sure of himself. The lecturer disliked excessive self-assurance in students. 'It should emerge from the patient's behaviour, his appearance and other factors.'

'Correct. Go on.'

'I would note how the history is given – either accurately and with insight, or in a roundabout, vague fashion. The state of memory would be easy to assess. Behaviour, neatness of dress and the simple sense of direction would all give an indication of the patient's state of mind, too.'

The lecturer nodded. Now, Harold was sure, he would try to trip him. 'You seem to have that well memorized. Let's jump about a little, just to see if you've absorbed more than a parrot's grasp of the procedure. Cranial nerves – what tests would you conduct?'

'Ocular movements,' Harold said. 'Facial mobility. Tongue protrusion and palatal movement.'

'Sensory tests?'

Harold frowned for a moment. 'I would test the position sense in the fingers and toes and the sense of vibration in the feet. I'd use the pin-prick test on the four limbs and on the face . . .'

'*Where* on the face?'

'The lateral spinothalmic tracts, sir.'

'That's right. Sit down, Legg.'

As he resumed his seat he felt cool sweat on his palms. So far, neurology was the toughest challenge he had come up against in his medical studies. That was why he had spent the larger part of the break studying textbooks and making notes on the subject.

Phillips, on the other hand, seemed to have spent the whole time boning up on the war, as usual. A few minutes later, as the bell sounded and Harold stood up and gathered his books, he heard Mike drop one of his observations to a girl student who had been too slow to get out of his way.

'Quite a New Year's gift the gallant lads gave us, wasn't it?'

The girl was mystified. 'What gift's that?'

'Recapturing Bardia, of course.'

Harold groaned, without realizing Phillips could hear. A moment later he felt warm breath on his face. 'Did I say something that displeased you, by any chance?' Phillips demanded.

Harold looked at him and shook his head. 'It was just the way you put it. Like a headline.'

It was clearer at every encounter that Phillips would like to have it out with Harold. Now, as the others left the lecture theatre, Harold found his way was being blocked.

'Excuse me, Mike. I'm in a hurry.'

'Just before the holiday,' Phillips said, squaring up to him, 'you sniggered at a remark I made about the Russian counter-offensive in Moscow. Don't bother to deny it. I heard you.'

Harold nodded. 'I remember. Another headline.'

Phillips narrowed his eyes. 'I suppose your popularity

with the lecturers makes you think you can sneer at anybody and anything.'

'I'm not all that popular with the lecturers, Mike. It's your unpopularity that makes it look that way.'

Phillips was transfixed on a dilemma. His constant desire for showdowns wasn't backed by any talent for handling them. He made a sour face at Harold. 'Headline or no headline,' he said, backtracking swiftly, 'can you seriously deny that Bardia was an important breakthrough?'

'No.'

'So you were just sneering for sneering's sake.'

'I didn't sneer. I groaned.'

'Why?'

'Because your so-called New Year's gift was kind of overshadowed by the Japanese invading Burma and taking Kuala Lumpur.' Harold tilted his head at Phillips. 'It's like making a diagnosis. You don't assume a cancer patient's doing well just because his ingrowing toenail suddenly improves.' Harold walked off while Phillips was trying to assemble a retort.

He hurried out of the hospital and across West Smithfield, hunching against the biting cold. There was less than an hour for lunch and it never seemed long enough. He crossed Giltspur Street and entered the small restaurant where they still served a ninepenny lunch, including pudding and a cup of tea. Judith was already there; she was at a table in the far corner, wearing civilian clothes. She waved as he came in.

Harold hung up his overcoat and went across. He kissed her cheek and sat down opposite. 'How are you?' He took her hand. 'It's been two whole days.'

She laughed. 'I'm fine. The Southwark Centre's a bit grim, but the ordeal's over and done with and I'm a bit wiser than I was.' She had been on a short course for ambulance nurses. 'How about you? Was the first day back at school as bad as you expected?'

'The first half was pretty taut. It'll get better this afternoon. We're visiting the general ops theatre.' He smiled broadly. 'Crazy, isn't it? Forty-eight hours and I was missing you desperately. Just because I knew I couldn't see you if I wanted to. I used to think I was in control of my emotions. But I've been terrible – grumpy as a bear.'

'I missed you too.'

The elderly waitress came to the table and asked for their order. Judith said she would have vegetable soup, Woolton pie and jelly with mock cream. Harold shrugged and said he would have the same. When the waitress had gone he sat back and gazed at Judith. They had been going out together for nearly six months. He still found it hard to believe his luck, or his timing. He had made his first approach to her at a point when her relationship with the houseman was crumbling. Since then, they had never seen each other fewer than four times a week.

He leaned forward and put his elbows on the table. 'God, I love you.'

Judith glanced across the room. 'Ssh. People can hear, you know.'

'Let them. It might cheer up the poor souls.'

The pot of tea arrived. As Judith poured, Harold said, 'What about next Sunday, then? Have you made up your mind?'

She was silent for a moment, then she said, 'Well, I've decided to do whatever you want me to do – if that's making my mind up.'

'It suits me, certainly.' On Sunday he would be twenty. He had suggested a celebration somewhere, just the two of them, then a visit to his father's house in Finchley, so that Judith could meet the family. 'Are you nervous about meeting them?'

'Sort of.' She put down the teapot. 'I just hope I don't let you down.'

'Don't be silly.' He sighed. 'I'm sorry it has to be done, really, but I'll get no peace until you put in an appearance. My sister's asked me every conceivable question. Keeps wanting to know why they've never laid eyes on you, after all this time.'

'It's bound to go better than your frosty reception in Fulham.' Judith tried to smile, but it was a memory neither of them could really find amusing. Judith's mother had been friendly towards Harold, but her father had snubbed him. For two very long hours – first during dinner, then in the parlour – the finicky, lip-chewing little man had maintained a stiff, silent hostility while Harold worked doggedly at pretending not to notice.

'Do you know, I thought it would be over between us after that,' Harold said. 'I simply couldn't see him letting you near me again.'

'He's a man of responses, Harold. There's no action in him at all. He's never encouraged or forbidden me to do anything – he's just approved or disapproved, since as long as I can remember.'

Judith had refused to believe that her father was against Harold because he was Jewish, even though Harold did suspect that. She was convinced that his open dislike was the result of a broken hope, one of many in his life; he had liked the young doctor she had been seeing before, and probably regarded Harold as an interloper.

'Let's not talk about it,' Harold murmured as the soup was brought. 'Let's wait until Sunday. If you don't get the reception I expect my people to give you, then I'll have grounds for getting moody. Until then – '

'You think there's a chance they'll disapprove of me, do you?'

'They might. I don't really think they approve of me. Not my mother and sister, anyway. I'm tolerated because I'm their flesh and blood. No other reason.'

Judith looked at him, her delicate face almost sad. 'You wouldn't let it make a difference to us, would you?'

'Would you?'

She shook her head. 'Of course not.'

'And I don't give much of a damn what they think, either. But still, we'll do the civilized thing, eh? No pre-judging. We'll present ourselves for appraisal as a nice, wholesome, well-matched young couple.'

When they had eaten lunch they walked to Holborn Viaduct and waited for Judith's bus. As it approached she squeezed his hand. 'Hope you enjoy the afternoon,' she said, kissing him. 'I'm going to have a trot round Fulham to try and find a surprise for your birthday.'

'You're a darling – I love surprises.' He held her close until the bus drew up, then released her and waved as she got on to the platform. He watched until the bus disappeared along High Holborn, then he turned and started walking back to the hospital. As he went, he hoped silently that Judith had a liking for surprises, too. Big ones. He had a beauty in store for her that he could hardly wait to spring.

On 11th February General Wavell, the Supreme Commander of all allied forces in India, the East Indies and the South West Pacific, sent a brief cable to Winston Churchill:

Battle for Singapore not going well.
I have given orders that there is to
be no thought of surrender.

General Percival, the British Commander in Singapore,

had 85,000 men on the island. Many of them were poorly trained and they were short of equipment. Even so, it seemed unlikely that the Japanese, with far fewer men, could really succeed in their plans to take the island.

The Japanese landings had begun, in darkness, on 8th February. By the morning of the 9th they held 20 square miles of territory. General Percival was shocked by the superiority of their soldiers, their firm leadership and the efficiency of their planes and pilots. He decided to destroy his oil storage tanks; he also made plans to abandon most of the island and defend the city at its northern perimeter.

The Japanese reached this line with disheartening speed. By the evening of the 11th General Percival's defence perimeter had shrunk to less than 28 miles. He knew the fight was over, but in obedience to Wavell's order he refused the Japanese demand for surrender.

On the 13th, the Japanese took the Western sector of the city. They seized control of the Alexandra Barracks where they slaughtered the staff and patients. Percival's troops, together with a million civilians, were now jammed into the city in an area of less than 30 square miles.

As shells and bombs exploded all around, hundreds of people died hourly. The stocks of British and Australian munitions dwindled. Water supplies were still coming through, but only at a fraction of the previous rate. On the night of the 13th fifty small British ships evacuated thousands of women and children from the island. They were intercepted shortly after by Japanese warships and forced ashore on the Indonesian Islands. Passengers and crew were then summarily butchered.

Wavell's order not to surrender was law; house-to-house fighting must continue to the end. But Percival was becoming desperately concerned for the population, as well as his troops. On the outskirts Japanese soldiers were murdering on a wholesale basis and torturing any prisoners they troubled to take. Women were being raped in the streets. The General tried to muster a concentrated counter-attack, but there was no room left for manoeuvre.

On the 15th, knowing how hopeless the situation had become, Churchill authorized Wavell to give General Percival powers of surrender if any further resistance seemed to be futile.

That evening, the General met the Japanese Commander, Lieutenant General Yamashita at the Ford Motor Factory on Bukit Timah Road. After some attempts to gain time, Percival was shouted down by the Japanese Commander. He was asked bluntly if he intended to surrender unconditionally or not.

'Yes,' Percival said. 'I do.'

In the following twenty-four hours 80,000 British Empire troops were taken into captivity by the Japanese. Among those captured was Private Albert Beale of the Middlesex Regiment. He was wounded and sick, scarcely aware of what was happening. His pal, Tim Lofthouse, explained what was going on as they were bundled together into the back of a truck.

'We're prisoners of war, Albert. The fighting's over.' Tim looked at the pale, weary, frightened faces around him. 'I reckon the Japs'll do for us, mate,' he whispered. 'No use expectin' mercy from them animals.'

Albert took it in through a mind-hazing fever and when he understood his predicament, he made a decision. Weak as he was, he would get at least one of the slit-eyed little bastards before they got him. One way or another, Lou and the kids would have some reason to be proud of what he'd done in the war.

7

'Of course, we're making great strides all the time,' Gregory Legg told Judith. He was standing with his back to the fire, arms folded as he summarized the current state of his profession. 'Because of the war and some of the unique clinical and surgical problems it's produced, we have to come up with answers at twice the usual speed. It can be very exhilarating.'

'I'm sure,' Judith murmured. She glanced at Harold, who was sitting beside her on the couch, almost glaring at his mother and sister. They were sitting opposite, mute and stiff, as they had been since he had introduced Judith twenty minutes before.

'Has your training touched on cardiology yet, at all?' Gregory enquired.

'Yes,' Judith said. 'We've been learning about chronic rheumatic heart disease and hypertension.'

'Fascinating territory. Hypertension's a lifetime study in itself.'

Harold knew this was a brave effort on his father's part and he appreciated it. Without the boring medical chit-chat the atmosphere in the room would have been twice as thick as it was already. He had no idea what the women's silent demonstration was about. He hadn't pulled any surprises; he'd told them in advance that Judith wasn't Jewish, or rich, or socially well-connected. He was getting angrier by the minute and wondered how long he could conceal it.

'I suppose you've already done some cardiac work, Harold?'

Dr Legg knew exactly the extent of his son's studies into the physiology and diseases of the heart, but Harold played along with the game and kept the talk going for another minute. He was on the point of changing the subject to something that would involve Judith more in the conversation, when he saw his lumpish sister yawn elaborately, flapping her hand at her mouth. Harold cut off what he was saying and stood up.

'Miriam. Can I have a word with you – privately?'

She gazed at him, all innocent bewilderment.

'You too, Mother.' He turned to Judith. 'Excuse me for just a minute. I'm sure father'll keep you entertained.' With his eyes he apologized to Dr Legg then crossed the room and held open the door. 'Come on,' he snapped. Pink with embarrassment, his mother and sister followed him out into the hall. He closed the sitting room door then marched straight to the kitchen and waited for them to catch up.

'Harold!' his mother blustered, her taffeta creaking as she stormed in. 'What is the meaning of this? Are you set on humiliating us? Is that what you're playing at?'

He remained silent and motionless until both women were close enough, then he banged his fist on the table. Miriam yelped with alarm.

'I've had to put up with plenty from both of you in the past,' he snarled, 'but this is the limit and I won't forgive you for it. Your behaviour in there has been disgraceful!'

'What are you talking about?' Miriam demanded.

'The scowling disapproval. The huffy silence. The yawns and fidgets and glances at the ceiling – your evil manners and total lack of grace, that's what I'm talking about!'

'How dare you!' His mother's voice was rich with outrage.

'Would you mind explaining it?' Harold looked from

one to the other. 'For weeks, *months*, you've been pestering me about Judith, wanting to know all about her, asking me time and again when you would get to meet her. So I bring her along and what happens? You both behave like I'd brought Goebbels' sister into the house!'

Miriam glanced at her mother, prompting her to say something. Her mother glanced back, her eyes suddenly reluctant.

'Well?' Harold glared at them, hands on hips.

'We know about that girl,' Miriam said.

'I beg your pardon?'

Mrs Legg had turned a deeper pink.

'Harriet Grossman,' Miriam said. 'She told us – well, she told mother.'

Harold blinked. 'What in God's name are you on about?'

'Harriet Grossman,' his mother said, dry-voiced, 'as I'm sure you know, has been working between the Charing Cross Hospital and St Batholomew's for the best part of a year. She's seen you at Bart's often, though she has the impression you've been ignoring her . . .'

'Every chance I get,' Harold snapped. Harriet was in her mid-twenties, a hospital almoner who lived three doors away with her mother. Harold had energetically detested her since he was a boy. She had enough defects in her nature to cripple her socially, and like his mother and sister, she was someone who surrounded herself with her Jewish faith and never stopped talking about it. Even in her work she specialized in handling the problems of Jewish patients. 'What has she got to do with anything?'

'This very afternoon,' Mrs Legg said, managing to edge the affront back into her tone, 'I was having coffee with Harriet's mother, and I mentioned, naturally, that you were bringing a young woman to meet us this evening.

Harriet was there. As soon as I mentioned that the girl was a nurse called Judith Martin, I saw the change in her face.'

Harold's mouth had dropped half-open as he listened. He could hardly believe he was hearing this. 'Judith knows Harriet. They spend a lot of time in the same wards. So what?'

The burden of revelation clouded Miriam's eyes. 'Do you know she used to be friendly with a young doctor?'

Harold nodded. 'Of course I do.'

'*Very* friendly,' his mother intoned, avoiding his stare.

'They spent weekends away together.' Saying it had almost given Miriam a seizure, if her appearance was any guide.

Harold wanted to do several things at once, most of them violent. 'So that's it.' He stared at his sister, letting her see how much he despised her. 'That mouldering cesspit Harriet calls her mind is a dead ringer for yours, isn't it?'

'Don't you talk to me like that!'

'She had a diseased imagination even when she was a kid – remember her running and telling you I was up to something in the shed with her sister?'

'That's got nothing to do with – '

'And you, of course, believed her.' Harold looked at his mother. 'Remember? She had you running down the garden in no time flat. And there I was, *in flagrante delicto*, showing the little girl my rabbits.'

'You're sidestepping the issue,' Miriam said sharply.

'There is no issue!' he shouted. 'You'd sooner listen to the poisoned gossip of that harpie down the road than hear an unmalicious statement of the facts.' He shook his head in exasperation. 'What difference would it make if Judith *had* been to bed with her previous boyfriend?'

'Harold!' His mother looked mortified.

'That's what you were both implying, wasn't it? Or did you mean they were stringing beads at weekends?'

'I don't like that kind of talk – '

'But sordid insinuation's quite in order, right?' He held up a finger at his sister. 'Listen, I know all about Judith's relationship with the doctor. *All* about it. It was the precise reverse of what you've been led to believe. And even if it wasn't, as I said, it would make no difference to me.'

Harold moved to the open door and paused. 'I don't say this to wound you, mother, I say it in plain vexation. Your Old Testament morality makes me sick. I can't take any more of it. I'm not going to live under the same roof with it any longer. I'll be out of here by the end of the week.' He strode off towards the sitting room.

The women looked at each other, their righteous distress overlapping. 'On his birthday,' Mrs Legg whined, 'he says that to me.'

Less than two minutes later Harold was leading Judith along the darkened street, apologizing to her, offering reassurance to cushion every apprehension and hurt.

'Was it the look of me, or what?'

'Don't be daft. If looks were anything to judge a person by, they'd have mistaken you for an angel.'

'Then what? The way they behaved, I'd have sworn I'd mortally offended them.'

'Judith, my worst fears were confirmed, that's all. You're not Jewish, so they can't accept you.' The lie was intended as a kindness, and it wasn't entirely a lie. They would never have thought so badly of Judith had she been of the faith, whatever her reputed history. His mother's distrust of gentiles, which had been passed on to his sister undiluted, was tribally entrenched and unshakeable. 'Still, it brought things nicely to a head. I've told them I'm leaving. I've wanted to for ages.'

'I feel terrible.'

Harold stopped for a moment to kiss her cheek. 'Try not to. I don't. As a matter of fact I feel rather good. I'm only sorry I put you through that.'

'I suppose it makes up for the way Dad treated you.'

Harold guided her round a corner. Judith asked where they were going.

'Somewhere nice.'

They walked in silence for a minute, then she said, 'It's been an odd day, Harold. All ups and downs.'

'I'd noticed.'

They had gone to a matinee of *The Maltese Falcon*, which they had enjoyed hugely. Afterwards they went to a restaurant and ate a terrible meal. Later they walked around Green Park in the fading light: that had been delightful, an hour when their pleasure in each other's company had swelled into a precious, idyllic isolation which they had been terribly reluctant to break. After that they had come to Finchley.

Harold stopped by a gate and felt for the latch. 'Here we are.' He led her along the path to a half-glassed front door, which he opened with one of the keys on the bunch he carried. They trod on old, scuffed carpet towards a dark varnished door. Harold opened it and went in first, switching on the light.

'What do you think?'

Judith looked round the modest, cosy room. 'Whose is it?'

'Uncle Leon's.'

'Isn't he in?'

'You'll meet him later – he's out working till nine.' He held up the key. 'I've had this since I was seventeen. A treasured possession. Whenever I've needed sanctuary, this has been the place.' He gestured to the settee. 'Take off your coat and sit down. I'll be with you in a minute.'

He went out to the kitchen and came back carrying a tray. There was a bottle of red wine on it and three glasses.

'I was determined the day would end right, whatever happened.' He set down the tray and opened the bottle with the corkscrew on his penknife.

'What if Uncle Leon doesn't like me, either?' Judith said it only part-seriously. 'That would really sink my self-confidence.'

'He'll love you. And you'll adore him.' Harold poured two glasses and handed one to Judith. 'Happy birthday to me.'

'Happy birthday, Harold.'

He sat down beside her, fingering the silver watch chain running from his buttonhole to his breast pocket. 'It's a lovely present,' he said. 'Just what I wanted.'

'You mentioned a watch chain so often I thought you were dropping hints.'

He grinned. 'I wasn't really. It's just something I've wanted for a long time.' He kissed her, then sat back. His face became serious. 'Judith, I wanted time alone with you, to talk about something important. It wouldn't have been appropriate earlier.' He waved his hand at the room. 'I wanted it to be done here.'

She sipped her wine, looking faintly apprehensive.

'You know the other thing I'm always talking about – setting up a practice in the East End?'

She nodded. 'That'll be a long time yet.'

'I know. Years. But there's a couple of other things I want to do. First, I'm determined to leave my father's house and work in an atmosphere of my own making. I don't want simply to be a doctor, I want to be a good doctor, and to do that I need to study very hard, and in the right environment. Tonight only made me more impatient to do it.'

'Where would you live?'

'I'm coming to that in a minute. I said there's a *couple* of things. The other one's as big as my ambition to work in the East End. Bigger, really.'

Judith frowned. 'Am I supposed to guess?'

'No. I'll tell you. I want to marry you.'

They had talked about it before. Twice. The first time, eight weeks after they had started going out, Judith had been undecided; she was sure she loved him – she confessed she had felt drawn to him the first time they met – but she thought it was too early to know what her feelings might be in the future. On the second occasion that the subject came up, she felt differently. They had been seeing each other for nearly four months at that point; Judith had told Harold that when the circumstances were right for them, there was nothing she wanted more than to be his wife.

Now she sighed. 'Harold, you're still a student. So am I. Neither one of us is settled enough . . .'

'Right,' he said. 'There's a lot of turbulence ahead, one way and another. I'm not talking about getting married just yet, darling. I'm talking about setting a foundation for the future. Something reliable at the centre of the turbulence.'

'What?'

'I want to buy a house. For us.'

The information startled her. She stared at him. 'How can you afford that?'

'I've got some money. My grandmother was generous to me in her will. I've never touched a penny of it. I could buy a place in the East End for next to nothing. What do you think?'

'I don't know what I think. Are you planning to buy one now? Move out of your father's place and move into your own – is that it?'

Not quite, he told her. He did want to leave Finchley and make a new home, but not in one move. There was a room for him, if he wanted it, in the residency at Bart's. He could put his own stamp on the accommodation and make it an ideal place to live and study. That plan was separate from the other.

His idea was first to buy an old house at the heart of a community he could serve. It would have to be cheap and it had to be large enough to provide a home and a surgery to work from.

'Something fairly rundown, but not derelict. A place that could be restored, bit by bit, so that when we're ready to get married, it's ready for us to live in.'

As he talked on enthusiastically Judith warmed to the propositon. She could picture them spending their spare time – such as they would have – making repairs, decorating, planning the furnishings. It would be a real home, something they would make together.

'How long have you been thinking about it?'

'Weeks,' Harold said. 'I decided I'd wait until my birthday before I said anything to you, though. What do you think of the idea?'

'It's still a bit big to cope with,' Judith said. 'But I think I love it.'

'Thank God.' He put down his glass and took Judith's from her, setting it on the floor beside his own. 'Come and kiss me senseless,' he said. 'This has turned out to be the best birthday of my life.'

He put his arms around her and pressed his mouth eagerly to hers. She struggled a little as he drew her over on to his lap.

'Harold! Don't!' She pulled back her head and looked at him. 'What if your uncle comes in?'

'If he comes through that door while I'm still in this mood,' he said, 'I'll kiss him, too.'

8

Gary Tucker had an obsession with the Crusades. Before that it had been the life and career of Genghis Khan, but at the time his enthusiasm hadn't bothered Jimmy Douglas, because there had been a kitchen utensil stall separating them. With the metal shortage, Percy Pavitt's Pots and Pans had gone into liquidation and Tucker's book barrow had moved up one, right next to the fish stall. Nowadays Tucker's compulsive chatter was a great aggravation to Jimmy.

'Capturin' Jerusalem – now that was the big achievement, Jimmy. It was the equivalent, say, of us takin' Berlin. It fulfilled the hopes of just about every European Christian.'

Jimmy's hopes had not been fulfilled – not that day, nor any of the other days he'd longed fervently for Tucker to drop down dead, or be run over, or just struck dumb.

'Yeah,' Jimmy muttered. 'I'll take your word for that.'

Nothing was right that day. It was freezing, for a start, with a deadly gale blowing in under the railway bridge. Jimmy had only a few meagre, unappetizing herrings and whiting on the stall, and something was wrong with his flask, because the tea had come out stone cold. To add to the misery, he believed his back trouble was starting up again. The aggravating presence of Gary Tucker was the last thing he wanted in those circumstances. But there he was, leaning on the stall as he had been for ten minutes, running off at the mouth about Pope Gregory and Saladin and Richard the Lion Heart. He couldn't even be insulted into silence.

'If I'd had a better start in life,' Tucker mused, casually sleeving a drop from the end of his purple nose, 'I'd have set meself up as a historian of that period. Straight I would. If I'd had the education, an' if I'd had the leisure . . .'

'An' if your auntie'd had balls she'd be your uncle.' Jimmy irritably nudged a fish box into line.

'I'm serious,' Tucker said. He had large, bleached-looking blue eyes that never seemed to blink. As he trained them now on the piles of second-hand books littering his stall, a regretful sigh steamed the air. 'All my life I've wanted to be a recorder – you know, gettin' it down on paper, everythin' I've learnt, things I've worked out for meself . . .'

'Why don't you go an' try it then?'

'I've got a livin' to earn, Jimmy. I don't have the time.'

A living, Jimmy thought. That was a laugh. Tucker made maybe ten bob on a good week. His books were all musty and tattered and stained. Even if they'd been in better shape he would have had a hard time selling them; they were about things people around there weren't interested in – science, politics, history – and just lately they were beginning to acquire a faint smell of fish.

Mercifully, a punter had arrived and was picking through the grimy stock. Tucker moved in, wringing his hands, nodding with modest pride at his collection. 'We have something for most tastes,' he said, smiling at the tall, thin, black-coated man who was handling the books with only the tips of his fingers.

'Just browsing, thank you.'

'If there's any special field of interest . . .'

The man shook his head. He pointed along the street to the houses beyond the pub. 'Is that Albert Square?'

Tucker nodded.

'I'm looking for a Mrs Beale. Do you know her, by any chance?'

'Right on the corner there.' Tucker said. 'Number forty-five.'

'Thank you.' The man nodded and walked away.

Tucker looked at Jimmy. 'Bit on the posh side, that one. Who d'you reckon he was?'

Jimmy shrugged. 'How should I know? Maybe it's something official to do with Albert.'

Tucker nodded. 'Poor old Albert.' He plumed another sigh into the air. 'It'd be a lot better if Lou knew about him for sure, even if the word's bad.'

It was the first thing Tucker had said all morning that Jimmy could agree with. 'Yeah. Missin' – that leaves her right up in the air. She hasn't a clue if he's dead, a prisoner or what.'

'She must be half out of her mind with the worry.'

They watched the tall man go round the corner towards Louise's front door. 'If he's bringin' her bad news,' Jimmy murmured, 'or if he's nosin', I hope he's brought his tin hat. Lou's temper's always had a short fuse an' lately it's got trimmed to nothin'.'

At the door the man rapped twice and stood back. As he waited he folded down the lapels of his overcoat, revealing a clerical collar. The door opened and he saw a thin young woman with soft, weary eyes that contrasted oddly with the stiff confrontation of her mouth.

'Mrs Beale?'

'Yes.'

'My name's Lambert. I'm new to this district – I'm a minister.'

'I can see that.'

'Could I have a few words with you?'

Louise closed her eyes briefly and grimaced, as if a wave of something unpleasant had washed over her.

'What's it about? I'm not religious, you might as well know that.'

'It's about your husband. I heard the bad news. And it doesn't matter to me if you're religious or not.'

She considered that for a moment, then stood back. 'I suppose you better come in.'

Lambert stepped into the hall and Louise closed the door. 'I'm in the kitchen,' she said. 'Feedin' my youngest.' She led the way through. As they entered the kitchen Ronnie looked up from the bowl of cereal in front of him on the table of the high chair. An instant before they came in, he'd been stirring it wildly with his spoon.

'Aw, you little devil.' Louise got a cloth and mopped the splashes off Ronnie's face and hands. He took it all without resisting, staring at the minister as he crossed and stood by the back door.

'What's this one's name?'

'Ronnie.'

The minister leaned forward and smiled. 'Hello, Ronnie.'

Instantly, the child became preoccupied with the pattern on the rim of his bowl. He stared at it as if it might burst into life any second.

'He's the shy one,' Louise explained. 'Not like the other three.'

'Are they at home with you? I mean none of them were evacuated?'

'They all live at home. Harry and Dora are at school. Kenneth's only four, he's through playin' in the front room.' Louise took the spoon from Ronnie and tried to feed him some of the cereal, but Lambert's presence had turned the child to a statue. He kept his lips tightly shut and his gaze fixed firmly on the bowl. 'He'll get round to it,' Louise murmured, dropping the spoon. She looked at the minister. 'Can I get you a cup of tea?'

'No thanks. Since rationing began I've stopped taking tea or biscuits or anything else when I visit people.' He pointed to the table. 'Shall we sit down?'

Louise sat by the corner nearest the high chair and watched Lambert compose himself opposite her. For the first time she noticed he had a scar on one pale cheek, running from under the ear to the corner of his chin.

'Has there been any more word?' he asked her.

'No. Just the telegram. Missing on active service. Possibly taken prisoner by the Japanese.'

Lambert sighed, examining his clasped fingers. 'Even in the Great War they took the trouble to write a letter.' He looked up. 'How are you feeling, now there's been time for it to sink in?'

Louise shrugged edgily. 'I don't know what I feel. It's different every other minute. An' nothin's sunk in. I don't have anythin' to go on.'

'Have you told the children?'

'No.' She had wanted to at first, but something stopped her. Afterwards, she had realized she only wanted to tell them because sharing the news was a way of spreading it thinner, making it easier to bear. She had no right to burden the kids like that, she decided. Her job was to protect them and keep them happy any way she could. 'They're best not knowin',' she told Lambert, 'until there's more to know.'

He nodded. 'Well, as you've no doubt guessed, I'm expected to visit people in the parish who find themselves in your position.' He was looking at his fingers again. 'I'm supposed to hand out comfort.'

Louise stiffened. 'How do you reckon to do that? There's only one thing'd comfort me. *You* can't lay it on. Nobody can.'

'I can try to make you feel . . . Well, not good, but less bad.'

'How?'

He was looking at her now, his eyes direct and steady. 'In your case, Mrs Beale, I wouldn't dream of suggesting prayer.'

'Just as well,' she said gruffly.

'Instead, I thought it might help some if I told you what happened to me.' He pointed to the scar on his face. 'I got this in 1940. Shrapnel. A bomb landed thirty feet from the house in Stepney where I was living at the time.'

'And you survived it,' Louise said sharply. It was bad enough he was here, she thought, trying to give her something he couldn't, without handing her his own hard-luck story into the bargain. 'I'm sure you went through a bad time, but – '

'The same bomb killed my wife and two children.'

Louise caught her breath. 'Oh, I . . .'

'Unlike you, I wasn't saddled with doubt. They were dead and I knew it. When the truth came through to me, when I stopped feeling as if I was watching and hearing everything from outside myself, I suffered more grief than I'd imagined anyone ever could.'

Louise was staring at him, wondering how a man like that reacted to something so terrible. On the day she received the telegram she had felt, at first, as if someone had put a hammer blow on her heart.

'You might think that religion came to my rescue,' Lambert said. 'But it didn't. I believed it had failed me. Every particle of me rejected the notion of God, I suddenly didn't believe he even existed. Then I entered a phase where I attacked myself, mentally and physically – I actually injured *myself*, Mrs Beale – for being alive and giving all that pain a place to happen.'

Louise knew what he meant. The children saw none of it, but in the privacy of her bedroom that awful day, with no need to sustain an appearance, she tore her hair and beat at herself like a mad woman. Twice since then something similar had happened; it was a sudden, wild grief that sprang from long brooding, an anguish that made her rage against her own existence.

'At least I've got something to pull myself round with every day,' she said. 'When I start feeling bad, I remember that Albert might be all right. I make myself believe he is. I've not been told any different, after all.'

'You're obviously a strong person. I don't think I am. After two years I still see their dear faces in my mind, and at times it brings me to tears. On the street I imagine I hear my daughter's voice, or my son's. But I *have* got over my loss to the extent that I care again about other people.' He smiled faintly. 'That's the small comfort I offer you. Whatever blow to the spirit you may suffer, whatever agony, it does pass, the worst that remains is occasional deep sadness. It's strange. You're filled with pain and despair for what seems an eternity, then one day you notice it isn't so bad any more.'

They talked for a few more minutes. Louise explained that she already had faith in time's healing properties, and in her own strength of will. She wished, though, that she had no need for either.

When it was time for Lambert to go, he stood up and took a card from his pocket. 'That's my address. If there's no one else to talk to, and you need to talk, drop in any time. I'm usually there.' Louise rose as he put down the card and went into the hall. She followed him to the door and opened it.

'It was nice to meet you,' Lambert said.

Louise nodded. 'Nice meetin' you, too.' She stood there for a moment, her lips moving slightly, as if she were rehearsing something before she dared say it. Finally she said, 'Did you start believin' again? In God, that is?'

'Oh yes. But nowadays I see Him rather differently.' He gazed across the square as he spoke. 'At first, I believed He was all-knowing, all-powerful. When I lost my family I went from believing He was uncaring to being certain He wasn't there at all.' He turned and smiled wanly at Louise. 'Now, I've a very calm certainty that He *is* there, and that He loves us. But I don't think He has the power to combat the evil we've created.' He took Louise's hand and shook it warmly. 'Goodbye, Mrs Beale. I hope you hear good news about your husband soon.'

She watched him walk away, then she turned and went back to the kitchen. Ronnie had almost finished his cereal. Louise ruffled his hair and sat down again, watching him eat. 'What did you think to the vicar, then?'

Ronnie gurgled something through a mouthful of food.

'Not a bad sort as that kind go, is he?' When Lambert knocked the door, she had been scared for a moment, wondering if all her doubt was about to be cancelled. Seeing a vicar, instead of a post-office messenger had been a relief, because she didn't believe she was ready yet to learn the worst, although she was inclined to expect it, for all her stubborn hope.

'Poor bugger,' she murmured, trying to imagine how terrible it must have been for the man to lose his family.

'Finished,' Ronnie piped, showing her the bowl. 'All done.'

'There's a good little lad.' And a precious little lad, she thought. They were all four precious to her, more so every day. She thought of the minister again and was overcome suddenly as she realized how much she hadn't lost. A moment later she reprimanded herself, sharply. What kind of woman was she, at all, to draw consolation from another person's tragedy?

* * *

Before Louise went to bed that night, she sat in the front room and listened to the news on the wireless. It was all the usual stuff, stories she felt she'd heard a hundred times before: near Burma the RAF had bombed Japanese supply dumps, reinforcements of British and Australian troops had reached Java, the Japanese had attacked the coast of southern Sumatra. None of it told her anything she needed to know, but she listened all the same. She knew it was daft, but she couldn't help believing that, one of these nights, she might get a clue about what had happened to Albert.

When she went to bed, she lay and thought of the prayers she used to say when she was a child. The last time she had prayed was just before TB finally killed her father. After that she hadn't believed in God any more.

Since talking to the minister, though, she was taken by the idea of a poor old soul up there in the sky, loving his earthly children but having no control over them any more. A kind, fallible God was preferable to a strong, vindictive, murderous tyrant who inflicted pain and suffering on good and bad people alike, without compassion. He was easier to believe in, too.

With her head down under the covers, Louise decided to offer a prayer to the revised notion of God. She whispered the words against the pillow, her hands clasped tightly at her breast.

'If Albert's safe, please try to keep him safe. If he isn't, please try to find a safe place for him. If he's gone then make him happy with you and let him know we all love him and always will. Amen.'

She turned over and curled up, wrapping her arms around her knees. As she waited for sleep she tried to imagine, as she did every night, that Albert was fast asleep at her back, breathing softly on her shoulder.

* * *

9

Food restrictions became tighter during the Spring of 1942. The butter ration for each person had been reduced to two ounces a week. The cheese allowance dropped to an ounce. People lucky enough to find eggs on sale were allowed one every two weeks, although children under five were permitted to have three a week.

The sixth of April was the day when white bread disappeared from British shops. A National Loaf was introduced in its place; it was greyish, fibrous and tasted, in the opinion of one disgruntled housewife, like starched cotton wool.

April sixth was also the day when the canteen at Bart's was closed down. Staff and students, thereafter, were expected to bring their own food. Because they carried it around with them, the students in particular were prone to take unscheduled snacks. On the morning of the eighth, during an unsupervised session in the Anatomy Room, Roger Lewis invited Harold Legg to share a Spam sandwich with him.

'Thanks, I will.' Harold lifted a corner and peeked at the filling. 'Since I've been doing my own cooking my stomach feels hollow all the time. I'm sure I'm missing something vital out of my diet.'

'That'll take care of the hollow feeling,' Roger assured him. 'If the texture of the bread's anything to go on, it'll probably plug up your stomach's drain hole for good.'

They were sitting on a long oak wall bench which ran the entire length of the room. On six porcelain dissection tables between the bench and the high-windowed wall opposite, half a dozen corpses lay in various stages of dismemberment. Aproned students milled around the tables, armed with probes, knives and saws, setting up a drone of talk as they whittled at the impassive remains.

'So how does it feel to be an attached person?' Roger asked. 'From what I gather, you've pretty well become engaged to the pretty Nurse Martin – in practice if not in fact.'

'It feels fine. Better than that. It feels terrific. I can recommend the condition.'

Roger shook his head. 'I don't fancy it. I don't even fancy women much any more, since the VD lectures. Still, I'll probably get over that.' He took a bite from his sandwich and pantomimed nausea. 'I assume you know why I wanted you to have some of this,' he mumbled.

Nowadays the two men saw more of each other, even though Roger was a year ahead of Harold. The training timetable had been reorganized to amalgamate practical classes wherever it was possible, in order to save on staff and facilities. In that room second- and third-year students were performing dissections; next door, third- and fourth-year people were learning to perform biochemical tests.

'How do you fancy your chances in the exams, Roger?' It was one of the frequently asked questions, idly put and never very seriously answered. The bonhomie of student life, Harold realized, was an amalgam of things like that. He wouldn't have had it any other way.

'I fluctuate between low confidence and despair. A month's cramming's going to be my only hope. You?'

'I'm putting in two hours of study every night. Sometimes three. I'm confident enough.'

'Swot.'

'I'm determined to make it,' Harold said. 'I've got firm plans for my future.'

'Plans have a way of evaporating. In two years time, you could be considering switching to law, or just taking to the road carrying a stick, with all you need wrapped in a spotted handkerchief tied to the end of it. I've seen a lot of students a year and two years ahead of me give up.'

'Why?'

'In the main, I think they just lose their relish for the profession. I can't blame them. Five years of hard bloody grind, and at the end of it you're nothing but a wet-eared houseman, sweating your cobs off day and night and getting stepped on by everybody.'

'I think it's worth it.'

Roger shook his head as he lobbed the remainder of the sandwich into a refuse bin. 'We're not talking about a five year course, or even seven, are we, Harold? You're the best part of a decade clambering about the medical foothills before you get to do any climbing.'

Harold slapped his shoulder. 'You're a real tonic, Roger.'

'Oh, I know. People have started calling me Mr Sunshine.'

They slid down off the bench and went back to their body. It was an elderly female with wispy white hair and pale, deeply wrinkled yellow skin. They were sharing the corpse with Lucy Burridge, a student in Harold's year. Lucy was performing a lung dissection; Roger's project was to make a fine-layered exposure of the tendons and blood vessels of the right hand, while Harold had been instructed to remove the heart and make notes on its structure.

Lucy glanced up from the gaping chest cavity and peered at them over her spectacles, which had slipped to the end of her nose. 'I'm making a mess of this,' she confessed.

'It can be tricky, getting a lung out in one piece,' Roger

said lightly, without offering to help. 'Especially an old lung that's got cemented in place with the years.' He lifted the half-dissected hand and stared at it. 'This is no picnic, either.'

Lucy put down her knife and pushed up her glasses with the back of her hand. 'She looks like a nice old person.'

'So quiet, too,' Roger murmured, poising his scalpel over a knuckle.

Harold was looking at the face. 'One of London's poor,' he said. 'Those are the special wrinkles of suppression and deprivation. Every line put there prematurely.' He picked up the small, gnarled heart and hefted it as if it were an apple. 'I'll bet this never had a lot to swell over. Just a pump, keeping her going from one miserable day to the next.'

'No lecturing,' Roger cautioned him. 'My social conscience is in good shape, and I'm sure Lucy's is, too.'

'My nationalist conscience is a bit shaky, though,' Lucy said, making another attempt at the lung. 'According to Mike Phillips, anyway.'

'Mike Phillips.' Roger pronounced the name as if it were the title of a terribly unpleasant disease. 'There's something far wrong with that lad.' He performed a delicate manoeuvre with the scalpel blade then looked across at Lucy. 'Has he tackled you about the Pacific War Council yet?'

'No. But I got an earful on the relative merits of British and American battle strategy.'

'It's a sickness,' Harold said. 'He can't talk about anything else but the war – and he doesn't really know much about it.'

'It's simply posturing,' Roger said. 'He wants to impress people – I'd say he's *compelled* to do it. He takes on a superior rôle to compensate for his fundamental lack of personality.' Roger had already let it be known, often, that he was keen on psychiatry. 'But he's like a man trying to impress people with his clothes, without realizing there's a hole in the arse of his trousers.'

Lucy nodded. 'Neat analysis, Professor.'

'And our poor Harold's got the same bug,' Roger went on, winking at Lucy. 'Forever playing the future saviour of the downtrodden.'

'It's better than going around with the delusion that I'm Sigmund Freud,' Harold muttered.

Lucy turned to him. 'Any luck finding a house yet?'

'No.' He made a glum mouth. 'I thought it would be easy, but so many places have been bombed, or the owners are unknown or temporarily unavailable. The really good buildings we've been offered, so far, are all in the wrong districts . . .'

'House?' Roger said. 'What's this about a house?'

Harold outlined his plans and when he had finished Roger nodded approvingly. 'Makes sense,' he said. 'For someone with your stable, saintly ambitions, anyway.' He put down his knife and lowered the lifeless old hand to the table. 'I think I can help you there, come to think of it.'

'Really?'

'There's an acquaintance of my father's, a bit of an entrepreneur. He handles the sale of big houses all over London, from Mayfair to deepest Dulwich. I could introduce you as a friend – that way you wouldn't be so likely to get gypped.'

Harold beamed. 'That's great. When can I meet him?'

'Today, if we get through early enough.'

Harold put the heart on a wooden dissecting block and began opening it with a sharp-pointed knife. 'You've made my day, Roger,' he said cheerfully.

On the other side of the room there was a yell followed

by a small commotion. As Roger watched, a slow, satisfied smile crossed his face. 'Phillips has just made *everybody's* day,' he said. 'He's stuck a suturing needle through his thumb.'

At ten minutes to five Roger's old Morris turned off Regent Street and drove along Conduit Street, pulling up in front of a doorway with eight different names painted on a plate alongside.

'I fancy he'll behave himself,' Roger told Harold before they got out. 'He owes Dad a few good turns. But we'll watch him, all the same. He doesn't respect anybody who won't haggle, and he could flog French letters to a monk.'

'I'll tread warily,' Harold promised.

When Roger told the receptionist who he was, they were shown in to the main office at once. Harold was introduced, Roger being careful to exaggerate the closeness of their friendship. Sidney Kane shook Harold's hand and told them both to sit down.

As Sidney was exchanging opening pleasantries with Roger, Harold took a quick inventory of the remarkable office. It reminded him of a West End cinema foyer. The carpet was a commotion of multi-coloured whorls. There was deep red plush on the chairs, a chromium-legged desk, gilt nude ladies supporting spherical lamps; on the flock-papered walls there were more than a dozen framed photographs of celebrities, all of them either hugging or kissing – in one or two instances both hugging and kissing – the man who now sat behind the desk.

'It's a funny old world we live in nowadays, and no mistake.' Kane said to Harold.

'It certainly is,' Harold said, without being too sure what the man meant.

'Nothing's the way it was. Nothing.' Kane was a Cockney who emphasized the fact with every measure he took to conceal it. He wore a light grey suit with a silken sheen, a pink and white striped shirt and a broad pink tie. His face was round and jovial but the eyes, Harold noted, were hooded, as if the lids were designed to conceal the hard bargainer lurking behind the sunny frontage. 'In what department can I help you, then?'

'I'm after a house,' Harold began.

'To rent?'

'To buy. I particularly want one in the East End.'

'Really?' Kane's expression suggested he found that astonishing. 'The housing business is in a bit of a mess at the moment, as you'll appreciate. I can have a place on my books in the morning and by afternoon it's only a pile of rubble. And *nobody tells me*. The shocks I've had, driving a prospective client up to a mountain of smoking bricks and plaster . . .'

'We'd appreciate anything you could do,' Roger said, pointedly glancing at his watch.

Kane nodded solemnly. 'I'm sure if anyone can be of help, it's me.' He pulled a fat leather folder out of the desk and flipped it open. 'Now if you'd been talking about something out Harrow way, or Northolt . . .'

'It has to be the East End,' Harold said.

Kane sniffed. He riffled his way to the back of the file, paused and frowned. 'In that area, I've details of five houses only,' he said. 'And of course, they may not all be there any longer. This particular sheet hasn't been updated for a while.' He copied the addresses on to a piece of paper and passed it to Harold. 'Take a look, anyway.' It was clear he wasn't going to offer transport when he was dealing with East End properties.

Harold thanked him.

'The price can be negotiated later,' Kane said. 'First, we'll see if there's anything you like.'

'What kind of price region are we talking about?' Roger asked.

Kane set his teeth and made a sucking sound. 'Depending on the size of the place . . .' He shrugged. 'Four hundred and fifty, five hundred.'

Harold stared at him. 'I was expecting to pay rather less than that. A lot less. I've seen them advertised at – '

'Seeing them advertised and getting hold of them are two different matters,' Kane almost snapped. He softened, realizing he had slipped into his bargainer's rôle too sharply. 'What I'm saying is, when you buy from me you buy a properly titled, legally airtight freehold. Through some agencies, you don't know what you're getting. You can even lay out your cash and get nothing.' He gestured at the folder. 'My prices are trimmed close to the bone as it is, given the amount of work I have to put in.'

Roger stood up. 'In that case, Sidney, maybe we'd better try someone else. Dad made a point of saying we should come to you, but obviously he didn't know your properties were beyond Harold's means.'

'Now who said that?' Kane's eyelids had lifted far enough to reveal fully the dark, lifeless pupils. 'Naturally, because Harold here is a friend of yours, and your father and myself have an association going back a long, long way, I would have knocked a bit off at the appropriate time.' He flashed an alarming smile at Harold. 'Now what kind of price were you thinking of?'

'Three hundred, tops.'

The smile died. Kane began to look as if he were sitting in something wet. 'Give me the list a minute, will you?' He took it and drew his pen through two of the addresses, then handed it back. 'On those three, we can probably talk terms.'

'I'll look at them on Saturday.'

'Fine.' Kane got up and saw them to the door. 'Give my regards to your father, won't you, Roger. Harold, nice to meet you.' The farewell was markedly cooler than the welcome had been.

On the way downstairs Harold nudged Roger. 'You really twisted his arm with the fib about your father.'

'When you're dealing with Sidney, below the belt's often the best place to hit.'

'Well, I'm really grateful to you. I hope we find something we like. Incidentally . . .' Harold pulled open the door and they stepped out on to the street. 'You only ever mentioned that your father's a Civil Servant. What does he do, specifically?'

'He's the Regional Inspector of Taxes,' Roger said, smiling affably as he got into the car.

10

'Well, at least milk's off the ration now,' Louise said. 'I can give the kids as much as they want.'

Queenie, the oldest of her three sisters, made a face at her. 'You're in here to relax a bit. Forget the kids an' the rationin' an' all the rest of it. Drink up, I'll get us another one in.'

That afternoon the Queen Victoria had received a large consignment of beer. Word had travelled fast. By seven o'clock the place was jammed with most of the adult residents of Albert Square, as well as people from all over the surrounding district.

'Two more halves of the best, comin' right up.' Gus had to shout to make himself heard. 'It's not been this busy since 1939,' he told Queenie as he refilled the glasses. 'Soon as the beer runs out, though, it'll be like a mausoleum again.'

'Drink an' be merry,' Queenie yelled at him, 'for tomorrow we'll be dry – eh, Gus?' She had already downed four halves of Luxford and Copley's bitter and her plump cheeks were glowing. She waggled her tight cap of curly hair, watching the effect in the mirror behind the empty spirit dispensers. 'It's ages since I felt this good. When the war's over I think I'll take up drinkin' in earnest.'

Gus nodded, sliding the frothing glasses across the bar. 'There'll be a few livers get ruined in here when peace breaks out.' He nodded towards the pillar where Louise was standing. 'How's she keepin', your sister? She ain't been about for a bit.'

'As well as you can expect, Gus. Bearin' up.'

Queenie picked up the drinks and went across to Louise. 'There y'are. Get yourself outside of that.'

Louise took a deep swallow and sighed. 'I must say it's a nice change. Thanks for draggin' me out.'

'I'd do it more often, if there was more places to go.'

'Well, the nights are gettin' longer. Folk can get out for walks in the evenin's.'

'I'm not much of a one for walkin',' Queenie said. 'Don't mind ridin' round in a nice car, mind you.' She leaned closer. 'I went to a dance in one last week,' she confided with a smirk.

'Where?'

'Over at Poplar.'

'Who did you go with?'

Queenie's eyes became veiled. 'That'd be tellin'.'

'If our Mum was alive an' knew about it, she'd pull your hair out.' Louise snapped. Queenie was married to a sailor who hadn't been home for two years. They had no children, but she looked after her elderly mother-in-law. Louise's sister Elsie and the other sister, Liz, had been dropping hints lately about Queenie not staying on the rails the way she once had.

'I'm not harmin' anybody,' Queenie said, frowning at the abrupt change in her sister's expression. 'An' I'm entitled to some enjoyment out of life, while I'm young.'

'I don't know how you can bring yourself to do it,' Louise said stiffly.

'Aw come on, Lou. Don't kid yourself. A girl needs a bit of fun now and again – I do, you do. An' like I say, it's harmless.' She took a drink from her glass. 'Who am I damagin'?'

'I don't need the kind of fun you're talkin' about,' Louise said stubbornly. 'You should be rememberin' your husband's away fightin' for his country. You could at least do him the courtesy of rememberin' your weddin' vows.'

'Do me a favour, Lou – don't preach at me.'

'You need preachin' at.'

'When my Alec gets back I'll be as true to him as any wife could be. In the meantime, if I nip off for a night out now an' again, it's only to stop me goin' off me nut with the loneliness an' boredom.'

'It's still no excuse for messin' around with men.'

Queenie turned away, huffily scanning the crowded bar.

Several local women – some of them girls Louise would have never suspected – were known to be 'carrying on' with other men while their husbands were away. One of them was in the same position as Louise; her husband was missing, presumed to be a prisoner of war. Louise could no more contemplate turning to another man than she could abandon one of her children. The impulse was entirely foreign to her.

'Look at that,' Queenie said, pointing to a huddle of people in the corner. At their centre was a woman of about thirty, chatting animatedly to two middle-aged men. She was heavily made up, sitting with her knees crossed in a way that revealed a provocative length of thigh. 'Now if you're talkin' about a real slut, that Tilly Pearson takes some beatin'. An' her old man's stationed on the south coast. He gets home regular.'

'The ones that run around are all *real* sluts,' Louise pointed out. 'Some are just sluttier than others, that's all.'

Queenie frowned. 'I could do with less of that, Lou.'

'I'm just statin' a fact.'

'Well, there's some might think you wasn't in a position to criticize.'

Louise glared at her sister. 'Meanin' what?'

'Rumours get about,' Queenie said airily. 'An' they don't get forgotten.'

Louise grasped her by the wrist and squeezed. 'What bloody rumours?'

'Ow! Chuck it! That hurts!'

'I'll tear your piggin' arm off if you don't answer me!'

'You an' . . . an' that Reg Cox.'

Louise's eyes widened. 'You filthy-minded cow!'

'It's what I heard.'

Louise nodded, scowling. 'From our Elsie. An' she got a bollockin' from me for it, after. Did she tell you that an' all?'

'Yeah, well . . .'

'There was nothin' in that business, you're a bitch to even think it. All he was doin' was movin' the barrow for me.'

'Well, you know what they say. No smoke without fire.'

They stared at each other for a moment, then Louise's hand suddenly shot out and cracked Queenie hard on the face. A dozen people in their vicinity stopped talking and stared. Queenie rubbed her cheek, hardly believing it had happened.

'That's nothin' to what you'd have got if we hadn't been in here!' Louise hissed. She was livid. She pushed herself close and addressed her sister through gritted teeth. 'Get this straight, an' remember it. You might see nothin' wrong in gaddin' about to dances and lettin' the odd bloke slip you a crippler in the back of his motor, but I do. We're different – you're a slut, I'm not. There's never been anythin' between me an' any other man, not since the day an' hour I wed Albert. If you ever suggest different again, I'll batter you purple. Now have you got that?'

Queenie stared at the floor, still rubbing her face.

'I'm talking to you!'

'Yeah, right,' Queenie mumbled. 'I've got it.'

'Right.' Louise emptied her glass and put it on the bar. 'I'll be off then.' She turned and pushed her way through the crowd by the door.

Queenie crossed to the bar, draining her glass as she went. 'I'll have another half pint, Gus.'

'Certainly.' As Gus bent by the pump he said, 'Nothing too serious, I hope?'

Queenie shook her head. 'Just a slap in the chops from me big sister. S'pose I asked for it.'

Gus glanced beyond her shoulder. 'If I take a couple of seconds longer to pull this, you might get it bought for you.'

Queenie turned and saw her brother Terence approaching from the door. As he reached the bar he nodded to Gus and gave Queenie's shoulder a squeeze. 'I'll see to that, guv, an' I'll have a pint meself.' He produced an ostentatious wad of pound notes, peeled one off and slapped it on the bar.

'Got nothin' smaller than that?' Gus asked. 'I'm runnin' out of change.'

Terence shrugged. 'Hang on to it, then. Just let us know when we've drunk it.' He turned to Queenie. 'What's up with our Lou? I spoke to her outside just then an' she cut me dead.'

'She's feelin' humpty.'

They took their drinks to a corner, where Queenie ran an openly critical eye over Terence's attire. He was wearing a dark green double-breasted suit with a chalk stripe, a green shirt and bow tie.

'Is it St Patrick's day or somethin'?'

'Don't take the piss,' he said defensively. 'This is the latest stylin'. An' it's not that reinforced wrappin' paper they usually make suits of these days, neither. It's the real thing. Worsted. Cost me eleven quid up West.'

Queenie dropped the corners of her mouth. 'You mean *you* gave *them* money? Not the other way about?'

'Now chuck it,' he warned her, 'else I'll have the drink back.'

As if she were taking the threat seriously, Queenie swallowed half the beer in three gulps. 'What brings you round here?' she asked him when she had recovered her breath.

'I heard about the beer arrivin'.'

She gave him a disparaging smile. 'Terry, I'm not as green as that clobber you've got on. Whisky's your usual tipple, an' you don't need to come in pubs to get it, what with your contacts.'

He made an evasive gesture. 'Thought I'd look in on Lou . . .'

'She's not in the mood for visitors.'

'Yeah, I guessed that a minute ago.' He sipped his beer. 'To tell you the truth, I was thinkin' of askin' Lou if she could put me up for a bit. I mean I couldn't ask you, knowin' the way Alec's old dear feels about me – an' Liz has got Elsie stayin' with her, as well as the kids.'

'How come you need somewhere to stay? I thought you still had your place over on Bristow Street.'

'I've had to let it go . . .'

Queenie read all the signs, the little behavioural marks she'd learned to translate when Terence was a boy. 'What kind of trouble are you in? Is it the law?'

He hesitated for a moment, then made the trace of a nod. 'Just a little misunderstandin'.'

'Christ, Terry.' Queenie shook her head. 'I told you already, you've been sailin' too close to the wind for a year now. Some of that stuff you've been floggin' could get you sent away for a hell of a stretch.'

'Look, they don't even know the name of who they're lookin' for. I'll be all right. I just need a place to put my head for a while.'

'Lou wouldn't wear it.'

'I'm not so sure, Queenie. She can be a bit tough an' sarcastic an' that, but the right kind of coaxin' can usually bring her round. She's family, after all. If I'm straight with her an' let her know I'm in a bit of bother, she'll see me right.'

Queenie emptied the glass and held it out to him. 'Take my advice, don't try it. Not unless you want your neck in a sling. She's changed a hell of a lot.'

'Since when?'

'Since just lately, I reckon. I don't know what it is, but her hardness goes deeper now.'

Terence sighed. 'What the hell am I goin' to do?'

'Well, you can get me another drink, for starters.'

11

The first property on Sidney Kane's list was at the end of a cul-de-sac in Hackney. Its steps were littered with rubble from the house next door, which had been bombed. When Harold and Judith had finally managed to get inside, they found both staircases broken and the sitting room floor cratered in three places. Four of the connecting doors had gone and the ones that remained fitted badly. Plaster flaked when it was touched; window panes were broken and the frames were split. In all, the house gave the impression of having died.

The second place was in Islington. It was larger than the first and from the outside it seemed to be in better condition. But when they got inside and Harold examined the floors, skirting and support beams, he arrived at a diagnosis which the smell in the place had strongly suggested when he entered: 'If the woodworm were to stop holding hands,' he said, 'the building would fall down.'

Their dejection lifted a shade when they saw the final property on the list. Number one Albert Square was a sturdy-looking end-of-terrace house, tall and narrow, with steps leading up to the main entrance and down to the basement door. It faced one end of the square's central garden, and it was close to the Victorian pub on the corner of Bridge Street.

'What do you think?' Harold asked Judith.

'It looks fine, from the outside. But so did the last one.' They walked around the side and looked over the wall surrounding the garden. 'There's a window open,' Judith observed.

'Oh, yes, so there is. I think we'll stick to the conventional method of entry, though.' He checked the list. 'Keys with landlord, Queen Victoria public house.'

Gus was wiping down the paintwork around the bar as they walked in. A couple of old men sat in the corner, playing dominoes. Otherwise the place was empty.

Gus nodded amiably. 'Morning.'

Harold nodded to him. 'Are you the landlord?'

'That's right. Gus Leonard, at your service.'

'We want to get hold of the keys to the empty house at the corner of the square.'

'Blimey.' Gus dropped his cloth on the bar and wiped his hands on his apron. 'I'd forgotten I had them.' He went round behind the bar.

'Has the place been empty long?'

'Yeah,' Gus nodded. 'Four years, thereabouts. It belonged to an old woman. When she passed away they locked it up an' that was that.'

'Have you any idea what condition it's in?'

'Never been inside,' Gus said, 'although the agent bloke who asked me to mind the keys said there's a bit of furniture still in there.'

Judith was looking around the pub, admiring the old fittings. 'Have many people asked to see the house?' she asked Gus.

'You're the first.' He ducked down behind the bar and stood up again after a moment, holding a bunch of keys. He handed them to Harold. 'What's your interest in the place, if you don't mind me askin'?'

'If it's in reasonable shape,' Harold said, 'I might buy it.'

'What, to live in?' Gus appraised the couple rapidly and decided they would be letting out the house. Nobody else around there dressed or spoke the way they did.

'That's right, to live in.'

'Oh.' Gus tried to conceal his surprise. 'Well, I hope it's what you're after.'

Harold thanked him and promised to bring the keys back as soon as they had looked over the place.

As they went back to the house Judith looped her arm in Harold's and squeezed it. 'I hope the place *is* all right.'

'You like it here, do you?'

She nodded. 'I've always liked Victorian squares. And the house does look friendly, doesn't it?'

For a time Harold had been wondering how Judith might respond to the reality of living in the East End. They had talked about it at length, and she had assured him she didn't mind where they lived, so long as it fitted with his plans. But talking about a place was a long way from experiencing it.

'There doesn't seem to have been much bomb damage around here,' Judith said.

'There's actually a lot,' Harold assured her. 'It's mostly on the other side of the borough, though.' He winked. 'The absence of damage hereabouts is maybe an omen. Albert Square could be a charmed place.'

At first, the big front door key refused to turn in the lock. Harold struggled with it, hearing rust grind deep in the workings. 'This omen I don't like,' he grunted. 'The house doesn't want to let us in.' The mechanism freed suddenly and the key turned with a sharp click. 'Ah.' He turned the handle and pushed the door open. 'Ready? Fingers crossed?'

Judith took his hand as they stepped inside. They paused in the hallway at the foot of the stairs while Harold sniffed the air.

'Can't smell anything,' he announced eventually.

They advanced along the hall, half expecting to find some terrible defect, but apart from the old, faded wallpaper and the scuffed paintwork, the place looked sound enough.

As they moved along Judith kept tapping the wall. 'Plaster's fine,' she murmured. At the previous house, she had managed to produce a foot-long crack with one sharp rap of her knuckles.

They entered the sitting room. There was a threadbare carpet on the middle of the floor; the boards around it had been painted brown. A fat old armchair stood by the fireplace and there was a small table with a dusty vase on top. Harold could already imagine what the room would be like with freshly distempered walls, painted woodwork and new curtains.

'It could be a nice, sunny room,' Judith said, mirroring his thoughts.

'It certainly could, darling. Let's not make plans for it just yet, though.'

They inspected the kitchen, which was spacious and looked on to the overgrown garden. Again, apart from the accumulation of dust and grime, there appeared to be nothing wrong.

'Upstairs,' Harold said. 'If there are any nasty surprises, that's where they'll be.'

They went directly to the second floor, where there was one large bedroom, a box room and a cupboard. Harold prowled around with Judith behind him. They touched and tapped and peered into every corner.

'Well, Judith,' Harold said eventually, 'I'm getting optimistic.'

She smiled. 'Let's have a look at the other rooms, shall we?'

They went down to the first floor. There were two doors. Behind one was the lavatory, housed in a space just big enough, Judith believed, to be converted to a cosy bathroom.

'So this'll be the main bedroom.' Harold opened the other door, took one step inside and froze. There was an old bed by the window; a man was lying on it, sound asleep. Harold and Judith looked at each other, then stared at the man again. He was fully clothed, lying on a spread overcoat with a raincoat half-covering him.

Harold rattled the door handle. Nothing happened. He rattled it again, louder. The man stirred and sat up suddenly, his eyes wide and startled. As he worked his tongue around his dry mouth he made an attempt to smile.

'I was, uh . . .' He made a helpless gesture with one shoulder. 'I wasn't doin' any harm . . . I let meself in last night, y'see . . . My van broke down an' I'd a bit of a distance to go. It was late an' what with the blackout, I didn't fancy walkin' all that way . . .'

'We're not the owners,' Harold said. 'We were just looking over the place. We're considering buying it.'

The man got off the bed and smoothed his hair. It occurred to Judith that he looked like a music-hall comic. He was wearing a green suit and shirt and a green bow tie hung loose on either side of his collar. 'I'm really sorry about this,' he muttered. 'I'll be on my way.' He started to do up his tie.

'There's no need to hurry on our account,' Harold assured him. 'If I'd been in your predicament, I'd probably have done the same thing.'

'Well, I've got to go, anyhow. I didn't mean to sleep this late.' He saw Harold glance at the two suitcases in the corner. 'They're mine,' he said quickly. 'I didn't want to leave them in the van.'

'When you're ready to go,' Harold said, 'you'll be able to use the front door. I've left it open.' He motioned to Judith and they went out.

'Bloody hell!' Terence muttered. He finished with his

tie and buttoned his jacket, then threw the overcoat and raincoat into one of the suitcases, which contained most of the remainder of his wardrobe. The other case was filled with cigarettes, coffee and boxes of Government-issue wristwatches.

He buffed the toes of his shoes on the edge of the mattress and put them on. Smoothing his hair again he looked at the heavy suitcases and sighed. Today, he swore, he would get himself sorted out. A couple of drinks, then he would tackle his problems head on and have everything settled by teatime.

He stood by the window for a moment, thinking. The first priority was to find a place to keep his stock; there was a lot of it, spread over three left-luggage offices and one suitcase. His best bet was a basement somewhere, in a house the police weren't likely to raid. Last night, after he'd remembered this empty house, he had let himself in and sat smoking in the dark for a while, laying plans to use the basement as a temporary store until he could locate something more convenient.

Now that people were coming and going about the place he would have to think again. There was also the problem of keeping his face off the streets for a while, until his description wasn't being circulated any more. He needed digs, with no questions asked, no curiosity being aroused. He stared across at Louise's house. Surely his own sister would help him, if she knew the score. In spite of what Queenie had said, he was beginning to feel just desperate enough to go and talk to Louise.

As he came down the stairs a few minutes later, lugging the heavy cases, he heard the young couple talking in the sitting room.

'I'm off, then,' he called to them. 'Sorry about all this.'

Harold came to the door. 'No trouble at all,' he said, smiling.

'Hope you'll be happy here, if you decide to take it.' Terence ducked his head in a gesture of farewell and shuffled out through the open front door.

Harold and Judith moved to the window and watched him cross the square. 'Quite a character,' Harold murmured. 'I wonder if he's wearing that suit for a bet.' He turned to Judith. 'Well, then. The house is all right, isn't it, and the area is just the kind I want to work in.'

'Are you telling me you've made up our minds?'

He tapped her nose gently with one long finger. 'No, I'm not. We decide together. The question is, do we decide now, or do we walk around the area for a while getting the feel of it, and then decide?'

'Well . . .'

'Or, do we do the terribly sensible thing and not decide at all, until we've gone away and taken plenty of time to consider everything in detail? We'll be determining our whole future, after all.'

'I'll tell you what I think we should do,' Judith said. 'I think we should lock up, take the keys back to the pub, have a drink if he's got any, talk some more and then decide we'll take the house.' She grinned.

'Darling, darling . . .' Harold put his arms around her. 'Be sure, now. Try to think of waking up in this house, in this square, most mornings for the next fifty years, say. Imagine how it will be to live and move in these rooms, to look out of this window and see precisely that view, year in, year out – '

'Harold,' Judith interrupted, 'I've already done all that. I like the place. I like it enough to fall in love with it in time. I love the notion of it being ours, and I'm thrilled at the idea of you making your career here. I've thought of it all, pictured it all – That kind of imagining doesn't take long.' She turned to the window and pointed. 'Look.

You can attach your plate to that pillar there, at the bottom of the steps.'

'And have an arrow pointing to the basement – that's where I'll have my surgery and exercise my astonishing skills.'

'While I'm up here, being a good little housewife.'

Harold laughed. 'We're like children, aren't we?'

'Yes, we are. And it's the way we should be.' She stood on her toes and kissed him. 'I think we're going to be happier together here than we ever thought.'

'Really?'

'Yes. Everything *fits*, Harold.'

He nodded. 'And from here on, if anything turns up that doesn't fit, we'll make it.'

Later, after they had inspected the basement and had gone all over the house one more time, they locked up and took the keys back to the Queen Victoria.

'What do you think of the place?' Gus asked them.

'We like it,' Harold said.

'Very much,' Judith added.

'Well, well. So we can be lookin' forward to havin' you as neighbours, eh?'

'One day.' Harold glanced at Judith and smiled. 'First we've got to get qualified, then married.'

'Qualified?'

'I'm training to be a doctor, Judith's a nurse. I want to set up in practice here.' Harold extended his hand to the landlord. 'I'm Harold Legg, by the way, and this is Judith Martin.'

Gus shook their hands and stood back, beaming at them. 'So we'll have a doctor in the square, eh? And a nurse. That'll be handy. We get quite a few casualties in here when trade's brisk.' He turned towards the door that led to the living quarters. 'I'll just nip up and get the wife. She'll love to meet you. We'll all have a little drink, eh? On the house, of course, just to say welcome. Shan't be a tick.'

As he disappeared Harold turned to Judith. 'I'd say that's a pretty cordial start to things, wouldn't you? I feel right at home, already.'

'So do I.'

Harold glanced along the bar to see if anyone was looking, then he put his hands on Judith's shoulders and gave her a quick kiss.

She smiled happily. 'It's just as I was saying, isn't it? Everything fits. We're where we belong, Harold.'

Terence knew about black pits of despair. He was familiar with cauldrons of loss and defeat, too. He had read a lot of Swan Library Historical Romances, sixpenny books that contained stories where ordinary events and emotions were rarely examined or even described. Everything in those yarns was scaled either to ecstacies and euphorias, or privation, failure and anguish, with nothing in between. Standing in Louise's front room, he found he was going through the kind of hell he had read about often, a scalding assault on his pride that threatened to leave him speechless.

As Louise paused for breath he did try to speak, though. His lips, as he ran his tongue along them, felt like paper. 'I only asked if I could stop here for a day or two,' he croaked. 'It's not as if I wanted somethin' off you. An' I can pay . . .'

'By God I know that!' Louise snapped. 'You've more money than the rest of your family put together, an' it's like everythin' else about you – it's rotten, crooked. I want none of it.'

'Our Mum would have helped me out,' he yelped. 'She wouldn't have turned her back on her own flesh and blood.'

'Don't you throw Mum at me! She was a good strong, generous soul, but she was easy taken in by you. That was her big weakness. Even when you were a kid, thievin' and lyin' all the time, she stuck up for you.' Louise jabbed a finger at her breastbone. 'I'm not Mum. I see through you. You're muck, nothin' less, an' I don't want you near here.'

It was hard for Terence to understand why she had turned so extreme in her dislike of him. Before, she had been scathing, reproachful and even loudly disapproving at times. But never anything like this.

He shrugged. 'If that's your final word . . .'

'No, it ain't.' Louise took him by the elbow and drew him to the front window. 'See that house over there? Number twenty-three? There's a man lives in there that's the worst kind of scum. He's a thief, like you. He's a swindler, just like you.' She turned her head and glared at Terence. 'In my mind there's nothing to pick between you. I wouldn't let him set foot in this house, and I wouldn't cross the road to spit on him if he was on fire. Same goes for you, Terry.'

He stared at her until he could withstand the hardness of her eyes no longer. 'Righto.' He turned and went through to the kitchen. He could think of nothing else to say, anyway, and he didn't think he could take any more abuse. It was best to shut up, get his bags and clear off.

Louise followed him and stood by the door with her arms folded. Terence picked up his cases and glanced at her. Her glowering, righteous expression put a feeble spark of resentment through him. 'I'd never have believed it, our Lou,' he heard himself say. 'Blood's thicker than water, when all's said an' done . . .'

Louise unfolded her arms and pointed out into the yard. 'See them kids? They're my flesh an' blood. Them an' my Albert.' She pulled open the door. 'Nobody else but them. Remember that.'

As Terence walked out, she stood in the doorway for a minute, her eyes distant as she gazed over the roofs at the bright sunlight making cracks in the clouds. In time they would all realize it; her little family was her life, and whatever the cost to other people's expectations, she wasn't going to open the doors of that life to anyone who could blemish it.

12

For Harold and Judith the year began to move swiftly. Days of hard work and study were followed by evenings – three, occasionally four a week – of cleaning, of paint and paper stripping, of replacing and refurbishing. Even though they kept reminding each other that they had years to complete the renovations, they worked long and steadily to bring the house in Albert Square nearer and nearer to the dream they had set down in notes and sketches.

The war moved faster, too, and there were signs of a change of direction. Chinese troops began hitting back at the Japanese. British fighter planes were stepping up the scale of their attacks on Libya. On the day it was announced that the Red Army was on the outskirts of Kharkov, Mr Churchill paid them a solemn tribute.

'I salute the noble manhood of Russia,' he said, 'now at full grips with the murderous enemy, striking blow for blow and repaying better ones for blows struck at them.'

At the end of his long speech he returned to his habitual topic of the British will to win. 'Here, in the thirty-third month of the war, none of us is weary of the struggle. None of us are calling for any favours from the enemy. If he plays rough, we can play rough too. Whatever we have got to take we will take, and we will give it back in even greater measure.'

In June there was a bitter setback. The British surrendered Tobruk, a vital sea port in East Libya, to the Germans after a long, hard battle. A month later, though, public morale was raised again when the commandos began making massive raids on Dieppe.

As American troops became a common sight in Britain, curious stories began springing up on the domestic front. Mrs May, the wife of the vicar of Worle, Weston-super-Mare, called together the women of the parish to lay down a six-point plan to ostracize black American soldiers, if they should ever reach the village. The women were advised, among other things, to cross the street if they saw a coloured soldier approaching. If they were in shops when black soldiers came in, they were to leave as soon as they were served, or simply walk out if they had been queueing. Above all, Mrs May emphasized, white women must have no social relationship, whatsoever, with coloured troops.

In responding to the story, the *Sunday Pictorial* of September 6th said that every coloured soldier must be reassured that he was as welcome in Britain as any other Allied soldier.

'He will find that the vast majority of people here have nothing but repugnance for the narrow-minded, uninformed prejudices expressed by the vicar's wife. There is – and will be – no persecution of coloured people in Britain.'

Christmas passed and fervent New Year prayers sought an end, before another year passed, to the war that had already made irreversible changes in millions of British lives.

Louise Beale faced the coming year with a stolid acceptance of her lot. There had been no more news of Albert but she still harboured some hope, deep down in her heart, though it burned much lower these days. She determinedly lived one day at a time, thinking neither forward nor – except in rare moments of weakness – back. She drew her warmth and distraction from the children, overseeing their lives and protecting them with a thoroughness that adequately compensated for the absence of their father. They were growing before her eyes, she often told Mavis Elliot. What she didn't say aloud was that it rather frightened her. Their dependent years now seemed preciously few.

In early February Louise's brother Terence was arrested in an Islington pub and charged with a number of offences, among them illegally purveying restricted and stolen goods for purpose of profit. In due course he was tried and sentenced to three years in prison.

Elsie called on Louise and tearfully passed on the news. Louise was unmoved. Terence had got no more than his desserts, she said. 'In fact I reckon he got off light with three years.' Grimly, she reflected that there was one other comeuppance she would have liked to hear about, though she didn't mention it to her sister.

To Louise's astonishment it happened, though not in the way she had wished, less than two months after Terence began his prison sentence. News got back to the square that a measure of justice had befallen Reg Cox. He had tripped on a gantry high up in a War Department warehouse and plummeted thirty feet on to a concrete floor. He now had a broken arm and two fractured legs. On top of that he had suffered a spinal injury and would have to wear a support jacket indefinitely.

Disliking the man as much as she did, Louise was guardedly surprised that she didn't feel glad about what had happened to him. What she felt, simply, was the satisfaction of knowing his black market days were over.

In the early summer Judith Martin took her final examinations and qualified as a State Registered Nurse. To celebrate, she and Harold decided to spend an evening in the Queen Victoria, where they now knew most of the customers. They sat in a corner, Harold drinking beer and Judith content with a glass of cordial, watching the clientele come and go and listening to the impromptu sing-songs going on at nearby tables.

After a while Judith nudged Harold. 'You're terribly quiet,' she said. 'You've hardly spoken since we came in.'

'Sorry. I've been thinking.'

'I don't know how you manage it, with this racket going on.' She leaned closer to him. 'Thinking about what?'

'All sorts. The house, for one thing. You realize it's nearly ready, don't you?'

Judith frowned. 'No, I hadn't realized.'

'Well, it is. Take away the ladders and dust sheets and buckets, throw out all the bits of old furniture that are left, put the new stuff in place and *voila*! you've got a home waiting to be occupied.'

'Mm. I suppose you're right.'

Their work had been speeded by the regular assistance of neighbours, who had helped to cart away the heaviest of the old furniture and to strip and clean the walls and woodwork. Gus Leonard and his wife had been particularly helpful. The couple were hoarders; they managed to uncover nine rolls of cream wallpaper in their attic, together with tins of paint and varnish. Gus and Harold had struck a deal over the materials, and one evening a week for the past two months Gus had thrown in his services as labourer, free of charge.

'Even the bathroom's nearly done,' Harold said. 'We only need to get the reconditioned boiler fitted and screw the mirror to the wall.'

Judith smiled. 'There we were, seeing years of work ahead of us . . .'

'It's the way we approach things, I fancy. If I've got a

job to do, I can't rest until it's done. There's no way I can be leisurely about it. I've noticed you're the same.'

Judith agreed with a nod. 'What else were you thinking about? You've been looking terribly distracted, you know.'

'I was thinking over an equation,' Harold said. 'The house is part of it. So's my family, and yours.'

'What do you mean?'

Harold clasped his fingers around his glass. 'I never see my people, largely because I took steps to make sure they kept their noses out. I'm something of a distant relative now. Your people aren't exactly close to you either, are they?'

'No. My mother just goes along with what Dad does. What Dad does is ignore me, most of the time. I'm a lost cause as far as he's concerned.'

Harold sighed. 'So there we both are, living separate, rather lonely lives – '

'Hardly that, Harold. We see each other every day.'

'But the background's cold, isn't it? You're alone when you're not with me. I'm alone up in my room at Bart's when I'm not with you . . .'

'What are you saying, Harold? What's the equation you mentioned?'

He swirled his beer. 'I think we should get married. Soon.'

Judith narrowed her eyes. 'Is that the beer talking?'

'The house'll be ready and waiting before we know it . . .'

'You could live there,' Judith pointed out. 'Better than Bart's, isn't it? And we did agree that we'd wait until we were both qualified before we got married.'

'Well – we're halfway there. Let's meet the plan halfway.'

'Harold, really . . .'

'Why not?' He took her hand. 'Maybe I'm twisting the picture a bit to suit my argument, but for weeks now I've been wanting to suggest this.' His fingers tightened on hers. 'Judith, I don't think my nerves would stand it, not two more years of imagining what it'll be like, the two of us together, in our own home . . .'

She looked at him with pursed lips, like a mother confronting a child she couldn't bring herself to scold. 'You're impulsive, do you know that?'

'Yes.'

'And it isn't fair of you to make unsettling suggestions like that, right out of the blue.'

'I suppose not,' he said in a small voice.

Judith tutted. 'I'd have to think about it. This tendency you have to spring things on me . . .'

Harold's eyes glinted hopefully. 'You're prepared to consider it, are you?'

She nodded. 'But this time, the decision will be reached after careful, serious consideration.'

'Whatever you say, darling.' He stood up. 'I'll get us another drink.'

He came back a minute later with the two glasses and set them on the table. As he sat down he heard Judith sigh. 'What's up?'

'Nothing's up,' she said. 'That was me bidding my spinsterhood goodbye.'

Harold's jaw dropped. 'You're saying you've – '

'After due thought and a careful weighing of the arguments, pro and contra,' Judith said, 'I've decided to fall in with your crazy suggestion.' She closed both of her hands around his. 'How soon shall we do it?'

13

They were married at the end of June, in a registry office less than half a mile from St Bartholomew's. Judith's parents were told well in advance. Harold had called on his parents and sister to tell them, too. Neither family turned up at the wedding. Uncle Leon, immobilized by phlebitis, sent a telegram congratulating them warmly.

The witnesses were Roger Lewis and Teresa Blair, a nurse who had been a friend of Judith's throughout their training. After the brief ceremony the couple, their witnesses and twelve friends from Bart's travelled in cars to Walford. A party had been laid on at the house and everyone in Albert Square had been invited.

'I'm beginning to remember what it was like before the war,' Roger told Harold as they sat down together on the second-hand couch. 'People relaxing without having to pretend. Laughter without the frown-lines. We were pretty happy-go-lucky people in those days.'

'It seems like ages ago, doesn't it?'

Harold looked across the room to where two women were holding on to each other's shoulders, giggling helplessly at something one of them had said. Near them two children were trying to imitate Gus and Flo Leonard, who were performing a foxtrot to Victor Sylvester's music on the gramophone. In a corner Judith was laughing, too, while a friend clapped a hand over her mouth and turned scarlet. The others in the room – neighbours, medical students and nurses – were wholeheartedly stepping aside from their daily lives and being irresponsibly happy.

'My God,' Roger said, 'Would you look at Mike Phillips.'

Phillips had been invited because Harold had felt a great generosity of spirit on the day he announced the forthcoming marriage. He had noticed Mike sidle away when he began inviting people. In spite of every memory of friction between them, Harold had to confess to himself that Phillips had become a feature of his life; he would never be able to think of student days without remembering him. So Mike Phillips had been invited and now he was enjoying himself.

'I've never seen him under the influence of drink before,' Roger said, grinning. 'It appears to suit him.'

Phillips was experiencing new aspects of himself. With an arm around one of the nurses he was concentrating, to the amusement of those around him, on learning a couple of dance steps. Every few seconds he would stop with his feet at odd, ungraceful angles and stare forlornly at his partner, then he would give way to a rush of laughter.

'He's just being who he is, for a change,' Harold said.

'It's a big improvement on who he tries to be, most of the time.' Roger put his hands behind his head, stretched out his legs and sighed. 'A party like this, once a week, would do us all a power of good. It would have to be in the East End though, wouldn't it? I get the impression these people have a talent for celebration.'

Harold nodded. 'On Sunday night we just went round the square banging on doors and telling people to come along. And look at them. Decked out in their best, generating fun. You'd think they'd been getting ready for this for weeks.'

'Who's the thin girl over there, with the kids round her? She seems a bit detached from the others.'

'Mrs Beale,' Harold said. 'She's a poor soul, really. Hardly any money and four kids to bring up on her own.

I gather her husband was listed missing a couple of years ago, just after the Japs took Singapore. She's had no news since.'

Roger stared at her for a moment, seeing the marks of chronic unhappiness, the distracted features imposed by countless days overshadowed by despair. 'I think I'll go and chat to her for a bit,' he said, getting up. 'She looks lost.'

As he moved away Phillips came across and dropped on to the couch beside Harold. He was panting and grinning, dabbing a handkerchief at his glistening brow and cheeks. 'Phew! I never realized dancing took so much out of you.'

'Enjoying the party, Mike?'

'It's the best one I've ever been to, old chap.' After a pause he added, 'Not that I've been to many.' He nodded at the table against the wall. It was laden with bottles of beer and spirits. 'How did you manage to get so much drink? I thought it was scarce.'

'We have a publican in our midst,' Harold said, winking. 'And I've been laying aside some whisky over the last couple of years, whenever I could get my hands on any. On top of that, most of the local people contributed a bottle. It all mounts up.'

'I've only drunk sherry, up until today. Never had beer before. It's rather good.' Phillips patted his stomach thoughtfully as he watched a pretty girl out in the hallway put two loud kisses on a short man's bald head. When he looked at Harold again his eyes were evasive. 'Um, I suppose I should say this, while I'm able to . . .'

Harold waited, noticing that Phillips' neck had turned pink. 'Say what?'

'Oh, just that I'm grateful to you. For inviting me. And I want to say how big-hearted of you it was, considering we've not always got along . . .'

'Mike, you're one of my mates. We don't need to look beyond that to the fine distinctions. You were invited because I wanted you to be here.'

'Dashed decent,' Phillips murmured, fingering his tie. 'Can't think when I last went anywhere . . .' Harold tensed himself for a gloomy, desultory flood of self-pity, but Phillips simply shook his head and said, 'There's just me and mother. It's pretty flat, most of the time.'

Across the room Judith was being counselled by Mavis Elliot, who had not only put on her best frock but was leaning on a newer, shinier walking stick than the one she normally used when her sciatica acted up.

'It's all very well lettin' men have their own way when they want it, lovey,' she confided in a near whisper, 'but if they're not made to wait, or told no from time to time, they turn into gluttons.'

Judith was managing to keep a straight face. 'I'll bear that in mind,' she said.

'I know modern girls are different from the way we was, but the old rules still apply. I had a good marriage, an' it was mostly down to me bein' firm about things – lots of things besides you-know-what.'

Judith asked how long Mavis had been married.

'Thirty-three years. They was all good years, too, right up to the end.' She put her hand on Judith's arm. 'Yours is goin' to be a good marriage, an' all. I can tell. You're right for each other.'

'I know we are.' On a surge of warmth towards the old woman Judith kissed her on the cheek.

Gus Leonard had stepped to the middle of the floor. 'Ladies and gentlemen!' he called. 'If I could have your attention, please.'

He waited with one arm raised as the talk and laughter died down. People came in from the kitchen and hallway; Harold crossed the room and stood beside Judith.

'Thank you,' Gus said. He cleared his throat loudly. 'I'm sure you'll forgive me for takin' up this time to say, on behalf of us all, how much we're enjoyin' this gatherin', an' I know you'll all join me in offerin' our sincere congratulations to the lovely bride and her lucky groom.'

A few cheers erupted. Harold had his back slapped a couple of times.

'We don't get a lot of excuses for celebrations these days,' Gus continued, 'so this is a precious an' memorable event. For meself, I'll always remember it as the day the Leggs got wed and came to live among us.' He turned and faced the couple. 'On behalf of us all, I want to wish you long life an' happiness in your new home.' He spread his arms wide. 'Judith and Harold – welcome to Albert Square.'

In the hubbub of cheering and handshaking and repeated good wishes, Harold turned and looked at Judith. She was crying with happiness. He put his arms around her and drew her close. The cheering rose again as he kissed her.

Louise Beale left the party early. She made the excuse that the children were getting tired, even though they objected noisily at having to go. When she got back home she placated them with some apples one of her old suppliers had given her.

'You lot be good, now. I'm just goin' upstairs a minute.'

In her bedroom she stood with her back pressed to the door, fighting down a feeling of panic that she had been holding under control, with difficulty, for nearly ten minutes. The party had done it, she knew that and she wished she had never gone.

'Just you steady on, girl,' she told herself. After a minute she started to feel better. The trapped feeling began to lift. She had warned herself, a year ago, that she should never go near anybody or anything that conjured the past too sharply. Today, sitting among all those happy people, she had been confronted with overpowering memories of her own wedding day, eight years ago. There were people at the Leggs' party who had been present when she and Albert were married. The voices, gestures, laughter and the bellowed congratulations were the same. The pattern of celebration was identical. It had finally become unbearable.

If the young man, the student, hadn't talked to her for a while, she would have had to leave much sooner than she did. For a few merciful minutes he distracted her from the pain of what was happening, keeping her mind occupied with finding answers to his posh-voiced questions.

She went to the dresser and looked at herself in the mirror.

'Oh, God . . .'

She looked terrible. Her eyes were sunken and the thin lines around her mouth looked much deeper than she remembered. She could never imagine that face smiling ever again. It certainly couldn't laugh.

She went back to the door and grasped the handle. The flashing panic had gone. The hopeless, no-way-out sensation was being replaced by her more usual – and manageable – grey awareness of the need to bear up.

As she opened the door and went out on to the landing she wondered how long she would be like that. She still remembered what the vicar had told her, that the worst became bearable after a while. She could believe it, but she suspected it only stayed bearable so long as she kept away from certain memories and echoes. It would be nice to think that, one day, she could really dwell on the past whenever she felt like it, without being reduced to a tangle of nerves and misery.

That evening the celebration moved to the Queen Victoria. Most of the students and nurses had gone home, but Roger Lewis was still there and so was a second-year nurse who had been receiving his attention more and more as the day wore on. By the evening they had reached a point of intimacy where Roger sat with his arm around her waist and she leaned her head on his shoulder. Harold and Judith sat alongside, talking to four of their new neighbours at once.

Around them the merriment continued unabated. Gus was demonstrating his talent with a melodian while Jimmy Douglas, the fish vendor, accompanied him on a tin whistle. Women, old and young, sang along and a few of them danced.

No one noticed the door open and a tall, silver-haired man come in. He was dressed in a dark pinstripe suit and carried a black leather briefcase. He paused and looked around, then crossed to where Harold and Judith sat.

Harold was explaining to a young mother how the virus of mumps is transmitted. 'It's carried by the saliva, you see. People catch it either by infection from drops in the air, or by contact with materials that have been contaminated by infected saliva. People often . . .' His voice trailed off as he noticed the newcomer. 'Father.' He stood up.

'I, ah, thought I should come along . . .' Gregory Legg mumbled awkwardly. 'To offer my good wishes.'

Judith had seen him by then. She rose and moved over close to Harold, her expression guarded.

Dr Legg nodded and smiled. 'Congratulations, my dear. You're looking very lovely.' He leaned forward and pecked her cheek. 'Can I look forward to you calling me Father from now on? Father-in-law is terribly stuffy.'

'Let me get you a drink,' Harold said. As he moved towards the bar his father grasped his hand and squeezed it. 'I'm sorry I couldn't come earlier. I truly intended to, but I've had four emergencies today, one after the other.'

'I'm delighted you came, anyway.' Harold stepped over to the bar and waved to attract Flo's attention. When she came he asked for a glass of red wine, which she took from the bottle Harold himself had supplied.

'For the gentleman, is it?' Flo asked, indicating her curiosity.

'Yes. He's my father.' Gregory turned. 'Father, this is Flo Leonard, one of our new friends.'

That introduction was the first of nearly twenty as the word spread and people began coming over to weigh up the kind of man Harold had for a father. Within ten minutes Gregory had been put thoroughly at his ease and was enjoying the carefree atmosphere as much as anyone. At only one point did his manner turn serious, and then only for a few seconds.

'About your mother and sister,' he murmured to Harold. 'I can only apologize for them. They're stubborn and woefully self-deluded, as you're well aware. Nevertheless, I'm sure their thoughts are with you.'

'I'm sure they are, too.'

Gregory allowed himself to smile again. 'I brought you both a present.' He took an envelope from his inside jacket pocket and handed it to Harold. 'It was the most practical thing I could think of.'

Harold opened it and took out a cheque for a hundred pounds. 'Oh, Father . . .'

'Don't say I shouldn't have.'

Harold leaned across to where Judith, Roger and the nurse were talking. He showed Judith the cheque. She read the figures and looked at Gregory. 'You shouldn't have,' she breathed, then wondered why her husband and his father began to laugh.

At nine o'clock Roger and his friend said they would have to be going. Gregory looked at his watch and announced he would have to go, too.

'I wanted to show you the house,' Harold told his father as they all moved to the door.

'Another time,' Gregory said. He smiled at Judith. 'I'm sure you'll want it to yourselves tonight.'

Harold and Judith stood on the pavement and waved as first Roger drove off, then Dr Legg. They faced each other for a moment before going back inside. 'It's been a perfect day,' Judith said.

'And you were the perfect bride.' He gave a little shiver, partly from cold, partly exhilaration. 'I can't believe my luck.'

Much later, after they had run the gauntlet of bawdy farewells in the Queen Victoria, they went home. Harold went directly to the kitchen and came back with a half bottle of champagne that he had possessed for three years. He uncorked it and poured them each a glass. Standing close to Judith in the dim-lighted sitting room, he proposed a toast.

'To you, my darling, and to the life we make here.'

They touched glasses and sipped.

'I feel like crying again,' Judith said.

'In a funny sort of way, so do I.'

Instead of crying they laughed, then Harold drained his glass and so did Judith, though more slowly. They looked at each other.

'I'm suddenly feeling rather shy,' Judith murmured.

'Oh, there's no need for that.' Harold drew her close and kissed her forehead. 'How can you possibly be shy with me? I'm going to be a doctor soon, remember?'

14

July and August were hot, dry months, a time of mixed blessings as Londoners toiled through long sunny days that tailed off into evenings of motionless air, darkening to humid, suffocating nights. In Walford, because of a shortage of man power in the Borough's refuse-collection service, streets were often rich with the mingling odours of warmed rubbish from a mounting tip by the railway embankment, and domestic pig-swill bins that remained un-emptied for days on end. At one point the smell became so potent that a group of wags in the Queen Victoria composed a ballad entitled, 'A Nightingale Choked in Albert Square'.

Judith and Harold Legg continued to work at St Bartholomew's for six days of every week. In the evenings, while Harold continued his studies in the sitting room, Judith spent every available minute in the garden. She cleared the dead plants, turned the earth, and in accordance with the Government's exhortation that the people should dig for victory, she planted row upon row of vegetables.The young couple had rapidly discovered a quietness and serenity in each other's company, a quality of unforced harmony that their neighbours had usually noticed only in married people who were much older. Residents of the area would watch them cross the square on their way home in the evenings, walking hand-in-hand, saying little to each other and invariably smiling.

'There'll never be a shortage of sunshine in the square with them two livin' in it,' Mavis Elliot had observed.

Others simply remarked that it did their hearts good to see such devotion.

That summer the war moved well in the Allies' favour. Italy had been brought to its knees and Mussolini was deposed. American troops had taken Messina, and a week later the Russians finally recaptured Kharkov. The Japanese had been driven out of New Georgia Island.

'It'll not be long now till it's all over,' Louise Beale told Harry and Dora one hot afternoon as they sat with her in the kitchen. It was their habit now to listen, for five minutes after school each day, while their mother passed on snippets of news from the *Daily Mirror*. 'Mr Churchill is seein' us through. He's in Quebec – that's in Canada. He's gone there to talk to the American president – '

'Mr Roosevelt,' Harry volunteered.

'That's right, love, Mr Roosevelt. Him an' Mr Churchill an' some other men are makin' plans to finish the war in the Far East.'

'That's where Dad is, isn't it?' Dora said.

'Yes, round about there somewhere.' Nowadays Louise didn't linger over questions that centred on Albert; as time passed he was becoming a dimmer memory for the children, anyway. Ronnie had no recollection of his father at all, and Kenneth had only a hazy, imperfect memory of the tall man with the sandy hair who used to carry him a lot.

'Does it mean Dad'll be home soon?' Harry asked.

'Maybe. We'll just have to wait an' see, eh?'

The subject changed as Louise gave them some more news, then the small ritual was over and they went out to play. Louise was left alone with her newspaper, which she always read at least twice, missing nothing.

Lately it had become a regular, soothing distraction for her to absorb all the news that had nothing to do with the war. If anyone asked, she could have told them the plot of Noel Coward's new play, 'This Happy Breed'. She also knew that the film 'Stage Door Canteen' was earning a lot of money, and so was 'For Whom the Bell Tolls'. She had read, with some dismay, that young girls in America were having hysterics and even fainting at the performances of a singer called Frank Sinatra.

Gradually, Louise was finding ways to accept her life with less grim and tedious effort than before. While she remained severely protective towards her children, her domestic territory and her privacy, she had gained a reasonable measure of calm from simple, routine activities.

There was a lot to be derived from the day, if it was used properly. She had the morning session with the newspaper before she took Kenneth and Ronnie out to the yard and played with them for an hour or so. There was half an hour, every afternoon, listening to Auntie Mave's reminiscences over a cup of tea. There was knitting, mending and a daily programme of house cleaning; there were long walks with the children and a storytelling period at bedtime. She had the BBC Home Service, too; she tuned in every evening and never missed an episode of her favourite Dorothy Sayers serial, 'The Man Born to be King'.

One afternoon in the last week of August there was a small variation in the routine: she had a visit from her sister Queenie. It had been months since they had seen each other. Queenie had changed, Louise thought; she was thinner and she seemed to be taking less care over her appearance.

'I didn't know if I'd be welcome,' Queenie said as she was shown into the front room. 'Seein' as we've had our ups an' downs, one way an' another.'

'There's not many welcomes handed out here nowadays,' Louise said. 'Nobody'll stop you comin' in, though.' She folded her arms and watched as Queenie sat down, fussily positioning her handbag on her knees. 'What've you come about, anyway?'

Queenie put on a hurt little frown. 'Do I have to come *about* anythin'? Could I not just be droppin' in to see how you're gettin' along?'

'I doubt it.'

Queenie fiddled with the catch of her bag. 'As a matter of fact there is somethin' – but I was goin' to come round anyway, even if it hadn't cropped up.' She seemed about to go on, then stopped herself. Behind the hesitancy Louise detected something else. It could be worry, she thought. Women who spent a long time fretting had a particular look in their eyes that nothing else put there.

'Well, I'm gettin' on fine,' Louise said. 'That takes care of that. So let's have it, whatever else brought you here.'

Queenie moved her lips back and forth across each other, as if she were spreading lipstick. Her eyes met Louise's then danced away again. 'I'm expectin', Lou.'

Louise took in the information and examined it. For the best part of three years Queenie and her husband had tried to have a family, without success. Queenie had finally decided she was barren. She had been certain of it, and that certainty had probably made it a lot easier for her to start running around with other men.

'You stupid cow.'

Queenie produced a handkerchief and dabbed at her eyes, although Louise could see no tears.

'How long?'

'Couple of months, I reckon.'

'Whose is it?'

Queenie shrugged. 'Hard to say . . .'

Louise's eyes widened. 'What? Are you tellin' me

you've been havin' it away with that many, you don't know who's the father?'

'For God's sake, Lou, you make it sound like I'm a whore!'

'A trollope, Queenie, a trollope. Whores get paid an' they don't get put in the club.'

Queenie's tears finally put in an appearance as she let out a wail and buried her face in her hands. 'What am I goin' to do?' she moaned.

'There's not a lot *to* do, Queenie. You just wait an' it takes care of itself. What your Alec's goin' to do when he finds out is somethin' else.'

Queenie's head shot up. Wet mascara spidered her eyes as she gaped at Louise. 'I can't have it!' she yowled. 'You don't think I can go ahead an' let it get born, do you?'

There was a long moment of silence as Louise moved close to her sister and leaned down over her, her face ominously taut. 'I'm a bit sick of havin' to throw my family out of here,' she said slowly. 'But that's what'll happen to you if you go on talkin' that way.'

As Queenie sat shuddering on her dilemma her face seemed to fall apart, feature by feature, until it was a crumpled mask of wretchedness. She began sobbing like a child, the tears running off her chin and on to her skirt as she gazed helplessly at Louise. 'Please, you've got to help me . . .'

'Why me, Queenie? What about our Liz, or Elsie? You're a lot closer to them than you are to me these days.'

'I can't tell them! I can't! They wouldn't know how to help anyway.'

'Oh.' Louise stepped back again, tightening her arms about herself. 'What special help is it I can give you?'

'You know about these things . . .'

'Liz has got kids, too – '

'Other things.' Queenie took a deep wavering breath. 'Bella Dalton, she was your best mate . . .'

'What's that got to do with anythin'?' Bella Dalton had become pregnant at the age of twenty. She had disappeared from Walford for six weeks; when she came back she was no longer pregnant.

'I thought maybe you knew what she did – how she went about it, I mean.'

'Listen!' Louise's bark was so sudden it made Queenie jump. 'I was only one of Bella's pals, I wasn't her best one, nor nothin' like it. But I know what happened, all right. She went to a quack in Shoreditch an' got herself minced up that bad she was in hospital for a month. It was touch an' go with that girl, Queenie. You want to try somethin' like that, do you?'

'I've got to do *somethin'*!'

'There's only one thing you can do. Have your kid an' face the music.'

'Alec'll kill me!'

'He'll do bugger-all of the sort,' Louise snapped. 'He might lay one on you, an' there's a good chance he'll walk out on you. But it'll be no more than you've asked for – an' you'll live.'

Queenie stared at the empty fireplace for a moment, then looked at Louise. 'Is that all you're goin' to say to me? In the name of God, I've come here desperate – '

'I've no magic answers. Nobody has.'

Queenie stood up and mopped at her streaked eyes. She threw one long, unbelieving look at Louise then went to the door and jerked it open.

'I'll tell you somethin', our Lou – there's not an ounce of pity left in you. You've turned into the hardest bitch I've met, bar none.'

'I've had to,' Louise said quietly.

Harold and Judith Legg were turning the corner into Albert Square when they saw Queenie storm out of number forty-five and go stamping off along Bridge Street.

'Rather a dramatic exit,' Harold remarked.

'I think she's Mrs Beale's sister.'

'Family squabble, most likely.' Harold squeezed Judith's hand. 'Part of life's rich tapestry. At least that's one problem we don't have to put up with.'

As they reached the house he went up the stairs ahead of Judith and performed his daily struggle with the door lock. 'Funny how there's always one job that never gets done,' he muttered, flinging the door open at last. He picked up the letters from the mat and took them through to the kitchen, dropping his briefcase on the way. Judith put her coat on the hallstand and followed him.

'Anything interesting?' she asked as she filled the kettle.

Harold methodically opened all four envelopes, then removed the contents. 'The books I ordered are out of print,' he muttered, dropping the first letter and unfolding the second. 'This is a bill from Maples for the chair we've decided we don't like . . .' He spread out the third letter and frowned. 'Oh.'

'What is it?'

'Talking of family squabbles,' he sighed. 'It's from my father. An invitation to dinner next Sunday. I can just imagine what that'll be like.' He looked at Judith. 'I could make an excuse, if you like.'

She shook her head. 'I think we should go. If only for your father's sake. He's such a dear man, Harold. He misses you, I'm sure.'

'Yes. When I was about the house at least he didn't feel so outnumbered.' He set the letter aside. 'I think we should sleep on that.' The fourth sheet of paper was another bill. 'I suppose that when I'm a doctor,' he said, 'my mail will be a lot more riveting.'

They took their cups of tea out to the sunlit garden, where Judith gave Harold a progress report.

'Over there,' she said, pointing to a cleared rectangular patch in the far left corner, 'I'm putting in bulb onions. It's maybe a bit late for planting winter radishes, but I'm going to try them anyway, in the other corner. And here . . .' She waved her arm towards a long narrow stretch that still had to be cleared and dug; 'I'm going to have lettuce and peas.'

'Where do you find the energy?' Harold moved close to her, inhaling the warm clean scent of her hair. 'You never stop.'

'It's the contrast that does it,' Judith said. 'Lately we've been dealing with a lot of soldiers and airmen. It's pretty depressing, most of the time.'

'I know.'

'So, when I come into my garden at the end of the day, it's great just to work at something that's . . . Well, productive, if you know what I mean.'

Harold slipped his arm around her waist. 'Everything you do is productive, Mrs Legg. You're a little wonder.' He kissed her cheek. 'What kind of productivity are you planning in the kitchen tonight?'

'I haven't decided yet. You don't mind if it's a bit late?' She pointed to the very first patch she had planted. 'I want to lavish a bit of attention on the beetroot and the dwarf beans.'

'I don't mind at all. I've got to spend an hour or so wrestling with the mysteries of splenic disorders.'

Judith wrinkled her nose. 'Not so much fun as beetroot and beans,' she said.

Later, as Harold leafed through his notes by the sitting room window, he glanced up and saw Louise Beale. She was sitting on a bench in the garden at the middle of the square. She had her back to him, but even so he couldn't mistake her mood. The slumped shoulders and bowed head were a badge of dejection he saw regularly at the hospital. As he watched she shook her head slowly.

'Poor woman.' He felt a small pang at his heart, thinking of the simple happiness suffusing his own life, comparing it to the cold cinders of Mrs Beale's existence. It pained him to see someone as lonely as her, so amputated from ordinary living.

He had to force his attention back to the notes. 'Tests revealing decreased immunoglobulins suggest extensive lymph disorders,' he read. 'Liver function tests, similarly, must never be underestimated.'

He looked up again and sighed, seeing Louise and simultaneously thinking of Judith working happily out there in the garden. When there were vegetables ready to be picked, he decided, he would take some across to the Beales, and would try to get some sweets for the children. It would be something.

Long after she had gone back to the house and had settled the children for the night, Louise sat in her front room, burdened with the same weight of pain that had clung to her since shortly after Queenie had left.

She had no clear idea why it was, but in spite of her anger and the way she had reacted earlier, Queenie's predicament had pierced her armour. She felt desperately worried for the girl. The more she reminded herself that her sister was a loose-living adulteress with nobody but herself to blame for the mess she was in, the more she recalled the times, throughout their childhood, when she had loved and protected that sister as much as she now cherished her own children.

If there had been means she could use to help Queenie,

Louise now knew she would use them, whatever the cost to her time and spirit. But she saw no way, none at all. All that lay ahead for Queenie was a life with most of its early promise cancelled.

'Same goes for Terry,' Louise whispered. And Elsie too, for all she knew. Liz was the only one of them who seemed to have escaped the larger pitfalls and disasters that littered the way forward.

Louise still couldn't feel sorry for Terence, shut up in his prison cell in Wandsworth. Yet for Queenie she had compassion that threatened to overwhelm her. That seemed odd, since as children both Queenie and Terence had been equally important to her.

She looked at the clock and saw it was time to turn on the wireless. She turned the knob and sat back, waiting for the old Philco to warm up.

As her mind slipped back to Queenie she found the answer to the mystery of her concern. It sat brightly at the front of her mind, as if it had been there all along. Terence had set out on a criminal path, knowing clearly that it was wrong; he was a thief and a cheat and had always known his villainy hurt somebody, somewhere. Queenie, on the other hand, tried hard to hurt no one, and had ended up by wounding herself terribly. The least she deserved was her sister's compassion.

Mystery solved, Louise thought, but it did nothing for Queenie. She leaned towards the set again, turning the tuning dial.

There was a loud knock at the door. Louise groaned. It was always the same. She could be on her own all day, yet when she wanted to settle down with the wireless she would suddenly be in demand.

She went out into the hall and opened the front door. She saw two men, their faces unclear in the shadow of the porch. There was a car parked by the gate behind them.

'Mrs Beale?' the one with the hat said. 'Look, I'm sorry about this, not letting you have any warning and so on.'

Frowning, Louise watched him put down a large bag. 'It's all been a bit of a muddle and rush.' He turned to the other man. 'Isn't that right?'

Louise stared at the hatless figure and felt herself sway sideways. Her elbow struck the wall.

'Take it easy, love . . .' The hatted man steadied her and moved aside, letting the other one step forward.

Louise could scarcely breathe. He was thinner, his hair looked grey and he stooped a bit. But there was no mistaking him.

'Albert . . .'

'Hello, Lou.' He came to her, smiling, and put his arms around her shoulders. 'It's me, all right. I'm home.' He drew her close, letting her tears warm the front of his shirt.

15

It took the rest of the week and half the weekend for the truth to penetrate and for Albert to realize he was truly back home. So much in the past two years had been dream, false hope and crushing disappointment. He had existed with an ever-present risk of death, both from his captors and from persistent, serious illness. He had grown to rely on nothing and to expect no freedom ever again. When the solid reality of family and home settled itself on him, when he could believe that captivity and despair were in the past, he sat alone in the front room and wept.

Louise came in and found him hunched forward in the chair. She knelt by him and put her arm across his shoulders, patting him the way she would a child. She said nothing, simply allowing the emotional spate its freedom to pass.

Her own acceptance of the truth had been swifter, but no less shattering. For hours, after the first flooding joy of reunion, she had been seized by physical and mental shock. It held her until the accumulated pain and foreboding withdrew, making way for the understanding that her man was with her again.

When Albert became calm again Louise kissed his cheek and stood up. 'I'll leave you to yourself for a bit longer, love.' She went out, closing the door softly, and returned to the kitchen. As she watched the breeze move the washing on the line outside, her mind drifted over the things she had learned in the past few days. If she had known the half of it before, she would never have expected to see her husband again.

After the first flurry of welcome, then the re-acquaintance with his family, and later his friends, Albert had sat down with Louise and quietly explained the chain of events that had come so near to destroying him, but in the end had brought him back to her.

He spent the early days of his captivity at a camp in Singapore. While he was there he was virtually starved; moreover, he was beaten several times by Japanese soldiers. The eventual outcome of hunger and prolonged punishment was a bout of pneumonia. He was transferred to a hospital camp where he remained for a month.

'That was the only proper rest I ever got,' he had told Louise. 'After that, right up till a couple of months ago, I was doin' forced labour, except for the times when I was too sick to work. If you were sick for more than two days they shot you, so I didn't take many breaks.'

For month after month he was shifted from one location to another, working on labour squads, building railways and military encampments. During that time he contracted malaria and beri-beri. Soon dysentery was added to his burdens, and once, for a whole week, he had mysteriously lost the use of one arm. Friendships were the most important moral props among the prisoners. Albert's moment of deepest despair came three days before he was shipped to New Guinea, when he stood by as a Japanese execution party decapitated his mate, Tim Lofthouse, for stealing food.

He had been transferred to New Guinea together with two hundred other British and Australian prisoners, to work on jungle clearance and the construction of an airstrip. Albert had no idea how long he was there. Bouts of malaria, interspersed with days when exhaustion often made him delirious, had taken away his ability to estimate time. Gruelling labour was punctuated by changes of site; he carried jumbled memories of being bundled into trucks, on to ships and railway wagons, times without number. The Japanese re-deployed their slave labour force so often that in time none of the men really knew where they were.

In late June the Americans sprang a massive surprise raid on New Guinea. The Japanese weren't prepared for combat on that scale; instead of fighting they took brutal steps to diminish the American victory.

'It was horrible, Lou. They ran round the place, screaming like animals an' shovin' their bayonets into every prisoner in sight. They killed more than a hundred before the Yanks got to them.'

When the American foot soldiers did arrive, Albert was among the prisoners who were presumed to be dead. He had been bayoneted and thrown on to a pile of corpses. But the bayonet had only penetrated the slack skin at the side of his chest, a legacy of malnutrition. He was bleeding, but the injury was superficial.

'I lay there for ages, gettin' weaker and weaker, until somebody noticed I was alive. The medics got me to one of their tents, then a doctor started workin' on me. I don't remember a lot after that, until they took me to the rehabilitation camp in the Solomon Islands.'

For six weeks the Americans had nursed him back to health. Then the bewildering business of repatriation began. He had long since lost his papers and his identity had to be checked and verified. The signals flew back and forward for days until finally he was told he was going home. He was put on board an air freight and flown to England in the company of a dozen other soldiers and six tanks.

'We got quite a welcome, wherever it was they landed us. Bags of food and beer. Pocketfuls of fags. Then when it was time for them to bring me home, somebody realized you hadn't even been told I was on my way.'

Now, thinking of how she felt when she saw him at the door, Louise was glad she hadn't been warned. There had been no such joy in her life before, and she doubted there ever would be again.

She turned as Albert came into the kitchen. It was still strange to see the change in him. The loss of weight had made him seem taller, and his eyes looked larger than before. He stooped because the muscles of his shoulders had wasted; his face was lined at the eyes and mouth, and his hair had turned almost white. He looked nearer forty than thirty-two.

'Sorry about all that,' he said, jerking his thumb towards the front room. 'It just came over me.'

'Nothin' to be sorry about.'

'I feel a lot better now, anyhow. In fact I'm feelin' pretty good, for somebody that looks like his own X-ray.'

'A bit of decent feedin'll take care of that.'

He came and put his arms round her. 'I was thinkin' I might take the nippers for a stroll.' He paused. 'Might drop in on Queenie, see how she is.'

Louise had said nothing to him about her family since he came home. He searched her face, interpreting her small frown.

'Do I get the feelin' that things aren't right with you an' your lot? None of them's been round since I got back. It can't be they haven't heard – half of Walford's banged on that door the last couple of days.'

'I might've put their backs up a bit,' Louise murmured. 'I've been hard on them, I suppose. It was the bitterness in me. Part that, an' part knowin' I had to be hard to get by.'

Albert nodded. 'I can understand that.' He removed his arms from her gently and propped himself against the door. 'Mendin' the fences won't be much of a chore, though.'

'Maybe not. The family's been gettin' itself in a right mess though, one way an' another.' She told him about Terence being in prison, and about Queenie's pregnancy.

'Christ,' Albert breathed. 'Terry's been askin' to get nicked for years, mind you. But Queenie – she'd be better off havin' a spell in prison herself, rather than this. Old Alec'll kick her backside off.'

'An' the poor kid'll get brought up with no dad, more than likely.'

Albert gazed towards the ceiling for a moment, remembering. 'About a month before we were captured, one of the sergeants got a letter, not signed or anythin', tellin' him his missus was muckin' around with a bobby.'

'Oh, Lord . . .'

'You've no idea what it can do to a bloke, Lou. He nearly went out of his mind. Tried to desert, just so he could get back an' kill the pair of them.' He sighed. 'It happens to a lot of men. An' even more of them worry it *might* happen.'

'Did anythin' like that ever cross your mind?'

He shook his head. 'Not once.'

'I'm glad, Albert.' She reached out and stroked his face. 'I reckon nothin' in the world could split us up.'

'Well the Japs had a go at it, God knows.'

'You know what I mean.'

'Yeah, I know.' He moved away from the door, rubbing his hands briskly. 'So, us bein' the solidest thing your family's got in their favour, what are we goin' to do about them?'

Louise was aware he knew the answer, but like a good teacher he wanted to hear it from her. 'A lot of sympathy and comfort for Queenie, maybe a few visits to Wandsworth to see Terry. It's the best anybody can do, for now.'

'Fair enough. I'll get the kids rounded up an' we'll go

over an' see your beloved sister. She can tell me the prison visitin' days while I'm there.'

Lou nodded. 'I fancy I'll come with you,' she said, noticing it pleased him.

Albert opened the back door. 'We've got to hand out what help we can, haven't we? It's only decent.'

Louise watched him go out to the yard and open the gate on to the street. She felt a sudden, trembling thrill at the sound of his voice as he called to the children. *He was back!* The awareness still hit her sharply at odd times of the day, and it still had the impact of a shock. Her Albert was home, and already he was putting his terrible ordeal behind him and getting set to do the decent thing by her dopey family.

She went to the hall to get her coat, realizing that she had forgotten how much it meant to Albert, doing the decent thing. On the other hand, she'd never forgotten how much she relied on his guidance in matters of common decency, and so much more. It was a blessing to know he was taking her in hand again.

16

On a cool, bright Sunday in September, Harold's Uncle Leon came to call at the house in Albert Square. He arrived laden with gifts – an enormous bunch of flowers, a jar of Marmite, several twopenny Mars bars, a packet of very rare Gillette razor blades, a new novel by Monica Dickens for Judith and for Harold a well-preserved gramophone record of the Bach Concerto for Oboe and Violin.

'The art of giving presents has taken a funny turn since the war started,' he said apologetically as he spread his offerings on the kitchen table. 'It looks like I've been doing some haphazard shoplifting, doesn't it?'

'It's terribly kind of you,' Judith assured him. 'I haven't been able to get Marmite for ages. And where did you find the Mars bars?'

Leon smiled, tapping the side of his nose. 'We old Jews,' he murmured, 'we know a thing or two about foraging. Bribery, too.'

'You're a treasure, Uncle Leon.' Harold put his arm around the old man's shoulder and led him to the window. 'See what my other treasure's been up to.' Judith smiled shyly and began fussing with the kettle and the teapot.

Leon had visited them only once before. Then, the garden had been a rocky, weed-infested little wilderness. Now, neat rows of vegetables flanked tidy miniature paths, and there were even a few flowering shrubs.

'Miraculous,' Leon breathed. He turned, looking out along the hallway, then around him at the bright-painted, fresh-smelling kitchen. 'You've made such a home of this place.'

'We've enjoyed doing it,' Harold said. 'Next year we're going to make a start on the basement.'

Leon turned his eyes to Judith. She looked almost childlike in a neat blue cotton dress with little white spots, her hair tied up at the nape of her neck. 'I boast about you, you know. Both of you. When the others are talking about their aches and pains, or the shortage of this and that, I go on about young Harold and his wife Judith, my two rays of sunshine – the future medical genius and the Florence Nightingale who could teach Mrs Beeton a thing or two.'

'Flattery's another Jewish trait,' Harold said, beckoning Leon towards the sitting room. 'Come and sit down.'

Leon took one of the chairs by the window where Harold and Judith often sat in the evenings, watching the gathering dusk. 'Judith looks more beautiful than ever,' he said. 'Marriage obviously suits her.'

'It's all a matter of finding the perfect husband.'

When Harold had put the Bach recording on the gramophone he came and sat by his uncle. For a minute they simply listened to the music, then Leon said, 'Your father was mentioned in *The Times*, yesterday. Apparently he delivered a dazzling paper to the BMA.'

'He let me read it. I'm glad it went down so well. It deserved to. Have you seen Father lately?'

'Last week.' Leon shook his head slowly. 'I was invited to dinner – the black sheep's bi-annual treat. God, the atmosphere in that house. It's stiff with posturing. Nobody ever lets their *spirit* show, Harold, or their personality for that matter. What they display is attitudes.'

Harold smiled dryly. Not long ago, he and Judith had suffered through a stifling session around his parents' dinner table. He was sure he could never go through with another one. He certainly had no wish to subject Judith to the ordeal again.

'There was poor old Gregory,' Leon went on, 'battling bravely to stay in the twentieth century, talking about politics, the war effort, the plans for a National Health scheme, and all the while your mother was cutting in with snippets about this Jewish benefit and that, and Miriam – well, least said, soonest mended.'

'Father told me she's started walking out with Lionel Jacobs.' Jacobs was a doctor, a few years older than Harold. Their families had known each other casually since the year the Leggs moved to Finchley. 'I can't say I ever thought of my sister being interested in men. It seems odd to think of her having sex glands.'

'Her and young Jacobs, they were made for each other,' Leon said. 'He was there last week, too. Do you know what the pair of them were talking about over dinner? The diaspora.'

Judith came in with the tea tray and set it on the table.

'What's that, Uncle Leon?' she asked him. 'Sounds like a flower of some kind.'

Harold smiled at her. 'The diaspora's the scattering of the Jews throughout the countries of the world,' he explained. 'It happened after they were sent out of Babylon. So my mother told me a time or two.'

'Miriam was talking about its effect on communal identity,' Leon said. 'Can you imagine how absorbing that was? I heard all about the challenge to traditional Judaism, about the resurgent interest in the *Torah*, and when she stopped for breath Jacobs chipped in with a lecture on how old laws should be preserved and obeyed intact.'

'Do you think they'll get married, Miriam and Lionel?'

Leon had no time to answer Harold's question. There was a sudden, urgent banging on the front door. Judith put down the teapot and went out to the hall. Harold was close behind her. She opened the door and found Albert Beale on the step, panting for breath.

'Sorry to disturb you, love,' he wheezed. 'Could one of you come, at all? To my place, that is. It's my sister-in-law. She's been taken bad.'

Judith didn't hesitate. 'Of course.' She picked up her little emergency bag from the hall table. It was for use during air raids, but so far it had been in service only once when she had dressed a cut on a local child's knee.

'You carry on,' Harold said to her. 'I'll just tell Uncle Leon what's happening. Be right with you.'

Judith and Albert hurried along to number forty-five. 'It happened very sudden,' Albert panted. 'She was sittin' there, just talkin', then she went white and started howlin' and clutchin' her stomach.'

Queenie wasn't making a sound as they entered the house and went into the front room. She was lying on the couch, pale and trembling. There was blood on her legs. Louise hovered beside her, balling up a towel soaked in blood. She had already tucked another one up under Queenie's dress.

Judith could tell straight away what had happened. She dropped to her knees by the couch and opened her bag.

'Your frock, love,' Louise said. She snatched off her apron and passed it to Judith, simultaneously jerking her head at the door, telling Albert he should wait outside with the children.

By the time Harold got there Judith had applied thick padding to contain the bleeding and raised Queenie's feet on cushions.

'Miscarriage,' Judith said.

'How much do you think she's lost?'

'Soaked two towels. A couple of pints, easily.'

Harold felt Queenie's pulse and peered at the pupils of

her wide, frightened eyes. The pulse was weak and fluttering. Harold spoke to her in a low voice, being careful not to sound accusing. 'Did you use something?'

She stared back at him, her lips clamped shut.

'It's important that we know,' he said firmly. The amount of blood loss suggested that the miscarriage hadn't been spontaneous. 'What was it you used?'

'A bit of bark,' Queenie said throatily.

'Bark? From a herbalist?'

She nodded.

'Is it still there?'

She nodded again.

Harold straightened. 'I'll try to raise an ambulance,' he told Judith. 'In the meantime, try to keep her from moving.'

Five minutes later an ambulance was on its way from the local hospital. As Harold walked back from the telephone box to the Beales' house, he remembered what one of his lecturers had said about people trying to solve their own medical and surgical problems: 'There is enough myth and misinformation loose in the community to guarantee that dozens die, every year, from the results of friendly advice.'

Harold wondered who had told Queenie about the bark. It was a method that had proved so risky over the years that even the back-street abortionists rarely used it. The bark came from the Slippery Elm. It was sold in herbal shops as an ingredient for various old-time remedies, especially cough mixtures.

Its more sinister use, however, was in the form of a small, flexible spike, no bigger than a matchstick, which was placed at the neck of the womb and kept there with padding. It swelled slowly over a period of days, gradually opening the womb until a haemorrhage occurred. Even if the woman stayed in bed during the process, the method was very dangerous. Queenie had obviously been walking about with the thing inside her, which was a suicidal thing to do.

Harold let himself into the Beales' house. When he looked at Queenie again she was much paler than before.

'Still a fair bit of blood loss,' Judith told him in a whisper. 'Even with the pads.'

The ambulance arrived while Harold was wondering if it would be too late. The woman needed surgery and she needed blood. She had been needing both for some time.

She was transferred quickly to the ambulance. Louise was told she could go to the hospital with her. Judith, Harold and Albert stood on the pavement and watched as the ambulance drove off. Judith turned to Albert. 'I'm afraid your couch is in a mess.'

'It gives us an excuse to get a new one, some day. I'll give it a scrub for now.' He smiled sheepishly. 'Thanks a lot for what you did. An' I'm sorry for thumpin' the door like that, must have scared the wits out of you. We was panickin' a bit. If you hadn't been here, God knows what might've happened.'

'It's why we came to live in Albert Square,' Judith said. 'To help.'

'And one day,' Harold added, 'we'll be able to offer a lot more help than we did today.'

'Do you reckon Queenie's goin' to be all right?'

'She looks a strong sort,' Harold said. 'But really, neither one of us is qualified to say. You'll know soon, though.'

Judith collected her bag and they went back to their own house. Uncle Leon had fallen asleep by the window. On tiptoe, Judith took away the tea tray and began making a fresh pot. Harold came into the kitchen and stood behind her.

'It's certainly been a different kind of Sunday,' he said.

Earlier, he had imagined a couple of hours of Uncle Leon's company, then a gentle mixture of casual study and plain idleness until bedtime.

Judith nodded. 'I hope she'll pull through. The blood was cascading out of her when I got there.'

'Mm. Poor, frightened, misguided soul. Before long, you know, we'll be handling little dramas like that every day.'

'And you can hardly wait,' Judith said.

'That's right, darling.' He reached out and put his hands on her shoulders. 'I can hardly wait.'

At the hospital, Queenie was taken directly to a theatre where she was given two and a half pints of whole blood and placed in a light, anaesthetic sleep.

Her bleeding was brought under control with clamps, then a surgeon painstakingly removed the embedded fragment of tree bark from her womb and stitched up the damage it had done. Finally the lining of the womb was removed, together with the three-month-old foetus, which had remained there in spite of the massive haemorrhage.

Queenie came round ten minutes after she was taken to the ward. She lay with her head and shoulders propped on two pillows. Her face was grey and sunken-eyed, the dry lips twitching as waves of nausea lapped over her. She looked slowly round the green-and-white ward, seeing other sick faces, hearing low, distressed moaning. Then she saw Louise, sitting beside her bed.

'How do you feel?'

Queenie closed her eyes for a moment. 'Bloody awful.'

Louise was pale too. For over an hour she hadn't known if her sister was going to survive. 'You look bloody awful, an' all,' she said flatly. 'But you'll mend, they tell me.'

They were silent for a few moments, then Queenie

said, 'I suppose you're going to tell me what a stupid mare I've been.'

'I reckon you know that without bein' told.'

Queenie moved her leg and winced as pain sliced across her abdomen. 'I didn't know it was dangerous. The woman that told me, she said it worked every time.'

'Oh, it worked, all right. Very thorough, it was. Nearly lost you every drop of blood you had.'

Queenie closed her eyes again. Tears slipped past the lashes and coursed down her cheeks. Louise was bending over her at once, running a gentle hand along her cold arm.

'Don't fret, love,' she whispered. 'It's over an' done, an' nobody'll be miscallin' you for it. You've been through plenty as it is. You've had more than your fit punishment.'

'I'm sorry . . .'

'Ssh.' Louise kissed her cheek. 'Just you rest, now. Try to sleep. I'll be back to see you tonight.'

Later, as Louise set out to walk the half mile back to Albert Square, she imagined how much hopeless misery Queenie must have been hiding during the past weeks. Since the day when they had all gone to see her, she had begun to show something like resignation. All along, though, the dismal spectre of her ruined future must have been crushing her.

That was all gone now, Louise reminded herself, the future could be a bright one after all. As soon as Queenie was out of hospital, Louise would see to it that she got herself properly on the rails again. She would look after that dizzy sister of hers until Alec came back to take over the job.

At approximately the time Louise crossed the road to take a short cut through a little park near the hospital, Harold Legg was settling down with his text books to do some revision. Judith was in the kitchen. Uncle Leon had left over an hour before, promising to call again the following Sunday, if he was free.

'I'm just popping out to the garden,' Judith called.

In the sitting room Harold had nodded absently. He found the chapter he had been looking for and flattened the book on his knees. One hour of study, he had promised himself, then he could relax with the gramophone on, or the wireless, or perhaps he would just settle down to read the Sunday paper.

'Fixing catheters,' he read aloud, impersonating the voice of his least-favourite lecturer. He leaned closer to the book, preparing to absorb the information. 'Phase One . . .'

There was a sudden, deafening bang that shook the house, then a roar as bricks and masonry began showering into the square. Harold found himself on his feet, feeling the floor shake, staring through the window as the flying debris hailed on to the pavements and went smashing through windows.

As the rumbling faded he went to the front door cautiously stepped outside. Thick clouds of smoke and dust billowed around the houses as people came out, frightened, bewildered by the damage. Harold went half-way down the steps and saw two houses at the opposite end of his terrace had disappeared. There was nothing there now but a mountain of rubble.

His alarm turned sharply to terror. He hurled himself back up the steps and raced along the hall. In the kitchen both windows were broken.

'Judith!'

He wrenched open the door and saw the ruined garden. Bricks, stones and slates everywhere. The earth was churned and pitted.

'Judith!'

He took two steps outside and stopped. Four huge

lumps of stone lay in the centre of the garden. A fragment of blue, white-spotted cotton protruded from behind them.

'God no! *No*!'

His terrified gaze danced over the rubble then stopped. Dumbstruck, his mind screaming, he stared through a vapour of coiling dust at Judith's half-concealed hand, the fingers curled lifelessly around a broken plant.

17

Although it was widely believed that no bombs had ever fallen within a mile of Albert Square, one had actually landed on the perimeter of the square in 1940. It was of the type known as a land mine, designed to be dropped by parachute and to explode some time after it landed.

On the night the bomb came down it had buried itself in soft ground near one end of the terrace where the Leggs eventually came to live. The impact of the landing had brought down the remains of a nearby derelict warehouse. The crumbling bricks, timber and plaster covered the crater and concealed every sign of the bomb's presence. In the general noise of the air raid, with explosions occurring every few seconds, no one had even heard the bomb land. In the morning, it was assumed the old building had been demolished by the fierce vibrations from direct hits in the surrounding areas.

Three years later the bomb was still there, under the rubble where grass and weeds had grown in profusion. As with so many others, its firing device was probably faulty. During the time it lay buried, the mechanism must have reached a critical point where the right level of vibration would trigger it. Someone had noted that shortly before the explosion in Albert Square, a train had rumbled across the bridge.

Ironically, the two houses that had been demolished were empty at the time. One had been run down and deserted for years, the other was unoccupied because the owners had gone to visit friends in Torquay. The only human casualty had been Judith Legg.

Harold was almost demented with grief. He would speak to no one. He shut himself up in bleak, harrowing confinement with his suffering. At times when the pressure of loss grew unbearable he roamed from room to room, like a beast trying to escape its pain.

He tortured himself with thoughts of how easily Judith might have been saved; if she had not gone out at that moment, if he had talked to her instead of poring over his books, if one single event of that day – any event – hadn't occurred, then probably she wouldn't have been in the garden when the bomb exploded.

His father attended to the funeral arrangements. Four days after she was killed Judith was buried in Walford cemetery. Although officially the service was attended only by close relatives, Harold's friends from St Bartholomew's and a few colleagues of Judith's stood in a huddle by the gates, participating from a distance.

Afterwards, Harold had only a memory of standing by the graveside, stunned, seeing his family beside him and Judith's parents opposite. The words of the service reached him but he didn't comprehend them. He recalled the sorrow on the others' faces, and he clearly remembered the cold, accusing stare of Judith's father. After the funeral, although his family tried to persuade him to stay at their place for a few days, he returned to Albert Square and locked himself away again.

Grief maintained its hold on him. For hour after hour he sat among Judith's possessions – her clothes, books, trinkets – touching them, wetting them with his tears as he tried to conjure her back from the things she had left behind.

Memories bludgeoned him and in sleep there was no escape. The dreams were vivid, full of her laughter, her energy, the sometimes perfect stillness of her presence.

Most punishing of all were the dreams of her warm-scented embrace.

One morning, two weeks after the funeral, Roger Lewis knocked at the front door. He went on knocking until Harold opened up.

'Hello,' Roger said. 'How are you?' He was shocked. Harold was unshaven and red-eyed. His hair was tousled and matted. He had lost weight, too, and in his grubby shirt and rumpled trousers he could have been mistaken for a vagrant. 'I expected to see you back at Bart's by now. We all did.'

'I'm not going back.'

Roger looked along the square. People were watching. Some of them had tried to rouse Harold a number of times, without any success. 'Can I come in? It's a bit public here.'

Harold stared at him for a moment, then reluctantly he stepped aside. Roger went straight to the sitting room and was shocked again by the mess the place was in. Harold shuffled in behind him.

'What do you mean, you're not going back?' Roger demanded. 'That's crazy talk.'

'Then maybe I'm crazy.' Harold had dropped into a chair by the window.

'You're one of the best students in your year. Think of the waste, will you? And what about all the time you've put in already? Are you going to chuck that away?'

Harold gazed at the floor, absently drawing his fingers over the stubble on his chin. 'I remember you talking about people losing their relish for medicine. Well, it's happened to me. I don't want to go through with the course.'

'I didn't think you were that weak.'

Harold stared at him. 'Weak? *Weak*? How strong does a man have to be, Roger? My life's core has been gutted out of me. Can you understand that?' He gulped back a surge of emotion. 'There's very little that means anything now. Nothing, in fact.'

'What about your ambition, all your plans to work in the East End? There was a time when you talked about nothing else.'

'That fire's died, along with all the others.'

Roger looked across the room. There was a framed photograph of Judith on the sideboard. He went across and snatched it up. 'What about her?'

Harold frowned at him.

'She backed up every hope you had. She *lived* for you and your ambitions. The pride you took in the way she supported you – has that died, too? If you'd any respect for her memory – '

'Her memory's precious to me!'

'Then revere it, Harold. Honour it by trying to be everything she loved you for.'

Harold waved his hand dismissively. 'That's just talk, Roger. Nothing but empty rhetoric. The reality I'm left with is a bit harder. My wife was everything to me. I realize that now. The hopes, the ambitions and all the rest of it – they relied on her being there, always. Now she's dead, so there's nothing left.'

Roger put down the photograph and shoved his hands in his pockets. 'Harold, I hate seeing you like this.'

'It's the way I am.' Harold turned and stared out of the window. 'I think you'd better go.'

Roger hesitated, wanting to say more, but he could think of nothing. Gregory Legg had warned him it would be hopeless trying to steer Harold round. He'd had to try, though. He waited, hoping Harold might say something he could latch on to, something that would give his argument leverage. But he remained as he was, staring into space. Finally Roger left.

As Harold's days continued to pass under an unshifting blanket of miserable inertia, world events rapidly became indicators of the way the war might end. The Russians had taken Smolensk and the British Fifth Army had control of Naples. The Germans and the Japanese were on the defensive in every quarter. The newspapers began advancing possible dates for an end to hostilities. Few of them doubted it would be soon.

At 45, Albert Square, there was renewed cause for rejoicing – this time on a small scale – when Albert announced that he had found work. The wage was nothing spectacular, but it would be steady. Added to his war pension it would amount to the kind of sum they could live on without, as Louise put it, having to pull their horns in too far.

The job was with the Admiralty, rebuilding office furniture that had been damaged in the raids, or had simply begun to wear out.

'I'll be on shellackin',' Albert explained to Louise.

'What's that, when it's at home?'

'You know – shellac, it gets sprayed on polished wood an' that, to protect the finish.'

Louise's pleasure at his news dimmed a little. 'What about your chest? I remember what some of them paint sprayers used to be like, coughin' an' barkin' all the time, turnin' to shadows before they was forty.'

'I'll be all right,' Albert assured her. 'I get to wear a mask. An' besides, it's only for now, until the war's finished. Then we can get the old barrow out again, eh?'

That was Louise's brightest dream. They talked about it often in the evenings, how they would widen their range, maybe develop the fruit side more. Perhaps even get a bigger barrow.

'Soon as this ruddy war's over,' Albert promised, 'they

won't see us for sparks, eh, Lou? Sky's the limit for Beales' Fruit an' Veg.'

'Whatever you say, love. As long as we don't have to go an' live up Park Lane, I shan't mind at all.'

On October thirteenth, the British people were elated to hear that Italy had declared war on Germany. Some time later, a day dawned when Harold Legg woke up feeling different. He lay still for a while, wondering at the change.

He had dreamt about Judith again, but by then the dreams were not locked to memory. Instead of heart-breaking images that recaptured a united, happy life, they were now grey landscapes where Judith had shared the predicament of Harold's loss. They communicated across cold, misty stretches of space that couldn't be closed. In those dreams she grieved over his dejection as hard as he pined for her. That night, he had heard her tell him to be strong. His strength, she said, was her only guarantee of peace.

He got out of bed went to the mirror. He couldn't remember when he had last looked at himself, but he was startled by what he saw. His beard had grown thick and patchy. His hair reached his ears. The dark-rimmed eyes and hollow cheeks completed the overall look of an emaciated, self-neglecting wretch.

As he put on the water heater in the bathroom he tried to analyse the change which, he realized, was quickening. The dream had been instrumental, to some extent. It was powerfully clear, closer to a mystical experience than an ordinary dream, and it had affected him deeply.

Harold grunted a small rejection as he wiped round the bath. He was cautious of putting faith in things like signs and portents. It was more likely that the reason for the shift in his feelings lay in a natural law, summed up in one of his mother's favourite Jewish proverbs: 'All things grow with the passing of time, except grief.'

There had been a point, somewhere in the senseless maze of days and nights since Judith died, when he had thought how disloyal it would be to let his anguish fade. It had also seemed impossible that it could. Now, he was tempted, almost, to accept that she was gone. It did not feel at all disloyal.

He bathed, shaved, and with a long pair of scissors he trimmed his hair. In a drawer in the bedroom he found clean underwear and a fresh shirt. With the heavy electric iron that had been a wedding gift from nurses at Bart's, he pressed a pair of flannels and smoothed the creases from his sports jacket.

He decided to clean the house and began by collecting all of Judith's things and packing them away carefully in suitcases and boxes. It was an act of farewell, he thought, but not of forgetting.

He spent three hours with gallons of hot soapy water, scrubbing brush, mop, broom and dusters, making the place as clean again and tidy as she would have liked it. After that he washed the grime from the windows, then decided he had earned a cup of tea.

In future, he realized, he would have to see to the running of the house by himself. Accordingly, he made a thorough survey of his domestic supplies. The sight of the kitchen cupboard made him smile a little. Even Judith's failings, he had once told Uncle Leon, leaned to the side of virtue. Although the Government discouraged the hoarding of food, she had laid in a good-sized store of tins and packets, adding to it at every opportunity, so that he would always have variety in his meals and would never go short. Lately he had survived on practically nothing, so there was plenty left. That evening he would cook a good, nourishing dinner.

He had to steel himself before he went to the garden, but when he did go out, the strenuous job of clearing the rubble was an adequate distraction. He was able to stand on the spot where Judith had died and feel a manageable sadness, with none of the devastating hurt that had dogged him all those weeks. He raked over the cleared earth and went back to the house.

Letters had been piling up. He took the bundle from the hall table and went to the sitting room with them. There was one from his sister and another from his mother. Miriam's was a turgid, overdone attempt to make him find spiritual strength through a renewal of faith. His mother's was rather florid, but it was gentler, even moving. To grieve alone, she wrote, was the hardest of suffering, but she understood his isolation. Besides, she pointed out, he wasn't alone; God was always closest to those whose hearts were broken.

'Your journey from happiness to misery was so short, Harold, and it will be a longer way back from your sorrowing to happiness again. Even so you will accomplish it, as long as you can reject despair. Draw such comfort as you can from knowing you are always in our thoughts and in our hearts.'

There was a curt note from the Teaching Faculty, asking when, if ever, he intended to resume his studies. Harold set that one aside for an immediate reply. There was a handful of rather painful official forms to be filled, all of them connected with his new status of widower. He put them aside for attention, too, together with a discreet circular from a monumental stone mason.

Towards evening his spirits began to feel low again. The tidiness of everything reminded him even more of Judith. He still couldn't move about the house without imagining she was there somewhere, just beyond, about to call out to him at any moment. He stood by the front window and remembered that dream. *Be strong*, she had said, *or I can never be at peace*.

Harold sighed. There was still a heavy streak of the sentimental Jew in him, he decided. But it helped. He strode smartly out of the room and went to the kitchen to make his dinner.

In the Queen Victoria a little after nine o'clock that evening, Gus Leonard looked up from his thinly-populated shelf and grinned with open pleasure.

'Harold!'

Several of the customers turned at the greeting. Their faces brightened, too. Harold looked very thin, but he was smartly dressed and seemed hearteningly sure of himself as he walked over to the bar.

'It's nice to see you, Gus.'

'An' it's a pleasure to see you.' Gus grasped his hand and shook it as Harold nodded to the others.

'What'll it be, then?'

Harold looked at the towel-covered pump handles, then at the sparse selection of bottles on the shelf. 'A brown ale, I think.'

'A brown ale it shall be, sir.' Gus opened the bottle with a flourish and decanted the frothing liquid into a glass. 'There we are. On me, that one.'

Harold thanked him. 'Cheers.' He had taken one sip from the glass when Gary Tucker, the street-market bookseller sidled up.

'Evenin',' he said amiably.

Harold nodded. 'Hello.'

'I was just thinkin' about you this mornin'. I got hold of a consignment of medical books, y'see. About twenty of them. They're the legitimate article, you understand. Not the kind of thing I can really let the public get their hands on. Would you maybe be interested?' His unblinking eyes fixed on Harold's face, beseeching an affirmative. 'I can do you a good deal, of course.'

'I don't mind having a look, although I've already got most of the books I'll need.'

'Well you never know, eh? I'll pop round here with them, if you like. Tomorrow night, maybe?'

Harold thought for a moment, then he nodded. 'That'll suit me fine.'

As Gary moved off to get a fresh drink another man approached Harold. Like most of the others present, he lived in the square. He was wondering about measles, which he believed his daughter was on the point of catching, although his wife thought it was more likely to be chicken pox.

Harold told him as much as he could, without actually seeing the child. As he talked to the man, he realized he was feeling better and stronger all the time.

Half an hour later, he knew that in one day he had travelled a long stretch of the road towards recovery. One by one neighbours had approached and engaged him in conversation. There was no commiseration, no trace of mawkish condolence. Before he knew it, he had a small crowd around him, each man determined to reinforce an increasingly obvious truth: life went on, and there was always room for a laugh.

As he was leaving, Gus called to him. 'Will we be seein' you regular again, Harold?'

'Yes, I think so.'

'Be going' back to your studyin' soon?'

'First thing next week, when I've done some catching up.'

They exchanged goodnights and Harold went out. It felt strange, walking back to the house alone. It would be even stranger, going in and knowing there was only him there.

But he could withstand it, now. He was armoured with his determination to take up the strands of what he had begun. As determination went it was still fragile, but it was hardening. And there was the warm reinforcement of knowing what those men in the pub had taught him, all over again. He smiled sadly, remembering that it was Judith who had said it first: He was where he belonged.

18

The first German V1 flying bomb landed at Swanscombe, near Gravesend, at eighteen minutes past four on the morning of 13th June, 1944. A few minutes later the second one came down in a field in Sussex. Later still one exploded in Bethnal Green and another in Sevenoaks.

It was a tame beginning to the onslaught which began in earnest two nights later. As 250 of the small, rocket-propelled bombs buzzed across the sky above London, somebody re-christened them doodle-bugs. The name stuck, and so did the memories of the devastation they brought.

In two weeks nearly three thousand of the weapons bombarded Britain, killing 2,752 people and seriously injuring 8,000 more. In spite of the D-Day landings in Normandy, all the talk about a swift peace began to fade. The Blitz was on again; as history repeated itself the people became resigned to the grim probability of more long years of war.

At the beginning of October Louise, Queenie and their other married sister, Liz, had their once-a-month get-together in the heavily blacked-out bar of the Queen Victoria. Nowadays Liz could get out on occasional evenings because her children were growing more self-sufficient. Elsie, on the other hand, scarcely went out at all, now that she had an at-home job stitching uniforms and making belts.

'It's piece-work,' Liz explained to the other two. 'Since she found out how much she can make if she really goes at it, she hardly lets up.'

'Always was a bit of a greedy bugger, our Else,' Queenie said brightly. 'Still, as long as it keeps her occupied, eh?'

The monthly gatherings served no special purpose, other than to bring all three up to date on what was happening in their lives. They had begun meeting like this at the beginning of the year; it was one of Louise's ideas for keeping Queenie on a narrower path, as well as giving Liz – a quiet, inward-looking woman – some kind of recreation.

'Look,' Queenie said, craning her neck to see into the other bar. 'There's that bloke Legg.'

Harold looked up from counting his change and nodded to the three heads poking past the partition. They smiled and sat back again.

'He's lookin' well enough,' Liz said. 'When's he gettin' qualified?'

'Next year,' Louise told her. 'He still reckons on settin' up in the square. It'll be nice if he does. He's the sort of chap you can talk to.'

'Terrible about his wife,' Liz murmured. 'Only married months, wasn't they Lou?'

'That's right. But it's more than a year ago now. He's put it behind him – an' he's seen plenty of terrible sights since then to harden him up a bit. Works evenin's in the Emergency Department at his hospital.'

Queenie shuddered. 'That must be horrible.'

Earlier in the year two doodle-bugs had exploded in the borough. Stories soon circulated about people running from demolished houses with arms missing, and others crawling out of the rubble on the bleeding stumps of amputated legs. A friend of Liz's husband was cut in two when a huge flying segment of shop-window glass scythed clean through him.

'Won't be long now till Terry's out.' Louise said, changing the subject.

'Next month,' Queenie confirmed, 'if he keeps his nose tidy.'

'That's one bit of good news, anyhow,' Liz sighed. 'There ain't a lot of it about.'

Louise looked at them both. 'I've been savin' a bit of good news for you, as it happens. I was waitin' till we got all the usual gossip over and done with.' She smiled rather secretively and took a sip of her watery drink.

Queenie stared at her. 'Well, are you goin' to tell us, or what?'

'Have a guess.'

'You've come up on the penny-points coupon.'

Louise shook her head.

'Somebody's died an' left you somethin'.'

'No, that's not it.'

'Aw come on, Lou,' Queenie complained. 'I don't like guessin'. What is it?'

'I'm expectin' another baby.'

Liz and Queenie looked at each other, eyebrows raised. Then they looked at Louise, beaming.

'If I've got it worked out right, I'm just about a month gone . . .'

'That's a bit soon to say for sure,' Queenie pointed out.

'Not with me, it's not. When I fall for a kiddie, I know it's happened, right away. It was the same with the four I've got.'

'Well,' Liz said, 'I'm pleased for you, Lou. It'll be a bit cramped at your place though, won't it?'

'A bit. But we'll manage.'

'How does Albert feel about it?' Queenie asked.

'I only told him this mornin'. I reckon he might be

gettin' over the shock by the time I get home tonight. But I'm sure he's as pleased as I am.'

At that moment, Albert was in the front room at home playing cards with Harry and Dora. The game was rummy, which he had taught them, and so far Albert had lost four games out of five.

Harry, who was eight now, had never liked being patronized by people. He cocked his head at his father as Dora shuffled the cards for the next game. 'Dad, are you just lettin' us win?'

Albert shook his head. 'You're playin' a blinder, the both of you. I haven't got a look-in, that's all.'

'I'm not playin' no blinder,' Dora flatly informed him. She was small and thin with dark eyes that observed him steadily from under her fringe. Dora could hand out reproach the way her mother did, with a sharp frown and a tightening of the corners of her mouth. 'You *are* lettin' us win. That's no good. It's not really like winnin' at all.'

'I promise you,' Albert said. 'I'm tryin' me hardest.' He looked at the clock. 'This'll have to be the last game, it's your bedtime.'

'Try an' win it, then,' Harry said.

It was a struggle, but Albert did win. The children begged him to play just one more game, but he was firm. 'Whatever it is you're doin', stop doin' it while you're looking good. That's my rule an' I'm standin' on it. Now come on. Up the wooden hill to Bedford.'

When he had seen them to bed and tucked them both in, he went back to the front room and sat down by the fire. Today his chest had been bad, his shoulders ached from standing spraying at the same angle all afternoon, and he had a headache from the smell of the shellac. Even so, he hadn't felt so cheerful, so downright *happy*, in a long time.

The thought of having another child had even interfered

with his card playing. The elation had clung to him all day, a shimmering bliss that still hadn't let go. He had made plans – it was mad, he knew, to tempt fate like that, but his head had been busy since morning.

The first solid plan was to build a new cot. The one they had was old-fashioned, spindly and unsteady. It should have been thrown away as soon as Ronnie grew out of it. There was some really lovely wood where Albert worked. It was spare, just lying about the place. The foreman was a good sort and Albert was sure he'd let him take what he needed. He would spend a lot of time on that cot. It would have every ounce of love and skill he'd got in him.

He planned to re-arrange the bedroom, too, so there would be space for the cot on Louise's side of the bed. While he was at it, he would brighten the whole house – some paint here, fresh wallpaper there, to welcome the new arrival.

He had even decided on a name, subject to Louise's approval, of course. If the child was a boy he would be called Peter. If it was a girl, then Pauline was the name Albert wanted her to have.

No one, perhaps not even Louise, could ever guess how much the news of her pregnancy meant to him. It was quite simply the best thing that had happened since he was rescued by the Americans more than a year before. It was an event of magnitude, for it had done nothing less than restore Albert's sense of himself as a man.

His impotence, which had shamed him deeply, was something he had never liked to talk about to Louise. She never raised the subject, either; not once did she complain or become moody about it. Tacitly they both accepted that, somewhere in the dark galaxy of cruelties he had suffered, his virility had been driven from him.

During the first few weeks back home, Albert kept telling himself that when he was better, when there was more nourishment in him and when he had taken more rest, he would be whole again. But he had stayed impotent until six weeks ago. Until then, when miraculously it just *happened*, he had been saddled with the conviction that he could never have sex with his wife again. But he could after all, and better yet, he could still father kids.

Bathed in contentment, he lay back in his chair and gazed dreamily at the fire. He began to drowse, the little plans and hopes dancing softly in his head. Then, perversely, his thoughts shifted.

'Dear God,' he sighed.

For a whole day his deeper worries about the war had slipped aside; now they were back, without being invited, and they presented him with a harsh new cause for concern. What kind of a rotten world was this to bring a baby into?

'They could flatten us in a week, with a bit of effort,' a man at work had said. He had a reputation for making accurate pronouncements where the war was concerned. 'Four heavy raids, say, one after the other. That would do it. The whole bloody place'd be turned to nothin' but rubble and dead bodies. It makes me sick to think about it. But you've got to face facts, after all. It could happen tomorrow.'

Even the few that survived would have a black time of it, for there would certainly be an invasion, and Albert knew what it was like to be the prisoner of an enemy who hated you. How could he justify creating a new human life at a time like this?

The following March, Louise was told that she might be carrying twins. Albert went through his elation and foreboding all over again. By now, though, there was less to worry about.

The Allies already had control of the west bank of the Rhine, and on March 23rd General Dempsey's Second Army crossed the river. On the twenty-eighth day of the month, although the people didn't know it yet, the last of the V-rockets fell on Britain.

In April the Russians reached Berlin. Two days after the shooting of Mussolini by partisans, the world learned that Adolf Hitler was dead.

WAR WILL END IN A FEW DAYS was the banner headline on three English newspapers. On 1st May the German Army surrendered on the Italian front. The following day Berlin surrendered.

On the third of May, amid the drama and the growing excitement of people preparing to celebrate the war's end, Louise Beale gave birth to healthy twins, a girl and a boy, in her bedroom at 45, Albert Square. It was only the third time that Harold Legg, now one month from qualifying, had attended a birth; it was the first time he had been in charge of the proceedings. In the unavoidable absence of the district midwife, Harold had been called in by a frantic Albert Beale and he had conducted himself, according to Louise, with admirably professional calm and certainty. Afterwards, Harold admitted he had been scared rigid.

In less than a week the war was over. Near Rheims, on the 7th of May, the Nazi General Jodl made the final capitulation of Germany to the American General Dwight Eisenhower. In London, the war ended as it had begun, with a fierce overnight thunderstorm. Weary citizens awoke and grabbed their clothes and torches, then realized there was no longer any need. They went back to sleep, building their strength for the VE Day celebrations.

All Britain rejoiced, and in Albert Square there was a

riotous open-air party. Every lamp-post was hung with flags and tables were set up around the central garden. Unexplained quantities of beer and spirits appeared; children were given paper hats and told to help themselves to cakes and buns that had been baked, during the past two weeks, from every ounce of flour and sugar the residents could find.

At the height of the celebration, shouldering his way through groups of dancing, singing, deliriously exultant denizens of Walford, Harold Legg took a zig-zagging route to number forty-five. He tapped the door and opened it.

'It's me,' he called. 'Harold Legg.'

'In here,' Louise called back from the front room.

He went in and found her on the couch, cradling a sleeping baby on each arm. She still looked weak, but she looked happy, too.

'It's a wonder they can sleep through all that,' Harold said. He came and sat beside her. 'I thought I'd look in and see how you are.'

'Oh, I'm doin' fine.'

'And Pauline and Peter?'

'Good as gold. An' sound as fiddles, thanks to you.'

'I just helped nature a little.' Harold reached out and gently drew the fold of the shawl away from Pauline's face. She slept with the solemn concentration of all babies, one tiny hand curled under her chin.

'Have you been enjoyin' the party?'

'I've had a drink or two, I'll admit, and I couldn't avoid getting caught up in some dancing.' Harold smiled. 'There's a party at Bart's this evening. I'm trying to save myself for that.'

'Well, see you have a good time.'

'I'll do my best.'

The door opened and Albert came in. 'Oh, sorry.' He

already treated Harold with the deference he would show a doctor. 'I'll leave you to – '

'No, no.' Harold stood up. 'I only popped in for a minute.' He crossed to the door. 'I'm off to have a drink with my uncle now, if I can ever fight my way out of the square.' He said goodbye to them both and left.

Albert stood by the couch, leaning forward to peer at the babies. 'Not givin' you any trouble, are they?'

Louise rolled her eyes. 'Does it look like they are? It's the third time in the last half hour you've been in to check on us. We're fine, Albert. You get back out an' enjoy yourself. I'll come out later on, if I'm up to it.'

Albert leaned lower and kissed her cheek. For a moment they held each other's gaze, hearing the laughter and music from the square. 'It's a great day, Lou.' Albert grinned. 'The new dawn, eh?' He straightened and went over to the window. 'It's not before time, either.' He watched two old women dance past, clinging to the arms of a soldier. 'We've all been through a lot, one way an' another.'

'Here's two that won't go through the half of it.' Louise drew the babies closer to her and looked up at Albert. 'From now on it's goin' to be a good life for all of them. The best they can have. I'll see to that.'

Albert turned to her, nodding. 'Me too,' he said softly.

'That's right, love. You too.'

The world's greatest novelists now available in Panther Books

Eric van Lustbader

The Ninja	£2.50	☐
Sirens	£2.50	☐
Beneath An Opal Moon	£1.95	☐
Black Heart	£2.95	☐

Nelson de Mille

By the Rivers of Babylon	£1.95	☐
Cathedral	£1.95	☐

Justin Scott

The Shipkiller	£1.95	☐
The Man Who Loved the Normandie	£2.50	☐
A Pride of Kings	£2.50	☐

Leslie Waller

Trocadero	£2.50	☐
The Swiss Account	£1.95	☐
A Change in the Wind	40p	☐
The American	75p	☐
The Family	£1.95	☐
The Banker	£2.50	☐
The Brave and the Free	£1.95	☐
Blood and Dreams	£1.50	☐
Gameplan	£1.95	☐

Peter Lear

Spider Girl	£1.50	☐
Golden Girl	£1.50	☐

Calder Willingham

The Big Nickel	£1.25	☐
Providence Island	£1.50	☐

David Charney

Sensei	£1.95	☐

To order direct from the publisher just tick the titles you want and fill in the order form.

GF781

All these books are available at your local bookshop or newsagent, or can be ordered direct from the publisher.,

---

To order direct from the publisher just tick the titles you want and fill in the form below.

Name ____________________

Address ____________________

____

Send to:
Panther Cash Sales
PO Box 11, Falmouth, Cornwall TR10 9EN.

Please enclose remittance to the value of the cover price plus:

UK 45p for the first book, 20p for the second book plus 14p per copy for each additional book ordered to a maximum charge of £1.63.

BFPO and Eire 45p for the first book, 20p for the second book plus 14p per copy for the next 7 books, thereafter 8p per book.

Overseas 75p for the first book and 21p for each additional book.

Panther Books reserve the right to show new retail prices on covers, which may differ from those previously advertised in the text or elsewhere.